BORN OF AN ECLIPSE

Other books by Katharine Johnson

Sylvie's Silence
Born in a Red Canoe
The Wind and the Drum
Mukluck Ball

BORN *of an* ECLIPSE

Katharine Johnson

SILVER FOX BOOKS

SILVER
FOX
BOOKS

CHAPTER 1

*At high noon the moon slid in front of the sun
and darkened the world.
Grammy beat her chest, pleading for the Sun God to return.
But the world remained dark.
Flora writhed in pain as she struggled to birth her baby.
At the moment of deepest gloom, a cry pierced the darkness.
Ahni was born!*

"Born bad!" Pap cursed. "Best we leave her for the wolves."

Grammy whispered, "Ooo-eee!" She beat her chest again, pleading for the Sun God to sweep away the darkness. Grammy lit cedar boughs. Smoke drifted to each corner of the little house. She lifted the boughs high and chanted over and over again, "Dark Spirits! Weaken your grip! Let light shine. Rule not the heart of this newborn. Darkness, I command you to shrivel and die. Have no power over this child!"

Little by little, the darkness faded until the sun shone brightly on the log house that nestled deep in a wilderness of forests, lakes, and steaming bogs. Grammy rejoiced. Darkness had been overcome. Light had won. She rocked the baby, brushing away her fear. Her granddaughter would not be ensnared by dark spirits.

Pap shook his head as he looked at the wrinkled and squalling baby. "Best if we leave her deep in the forest right away."

"No!" Grammy held the baby girl to her bosom. "We will not leave her in the forest! We will love her. You'll see. I chased the darkness away before it had time to clutch our little one. She is safe and not born bad."

Flora mopped the beads of sweat from her forehead. The birth had been hard, and she'd moaned in pain more than once. Now, she wept silently as the two argued. She'd long wanted a child, but not one born during an eclipse.

"I take her now." Pap reached for the baby wrapped in old aprons and skirts. "Now! Before she fills her first bottom rag. The forest creatures will know what to do with her, and we won't have to live in fear always wondering what evil she'll bring upon us."

Grammy held onto the newborn. "Never! I will not let her go. Listen. She has stopped her wailing. She is a good girl. The cursed eclipse did not mar her. Look how perfect she is."

Even though she'd been born during the solar eclipse, Ahni's Mam and Grammy treasured her, loved her, cuddled her, and thought she was the most precious little tyke ever. Even though her face was pinched and red when she was born, they took turns swaddling her and stroking her soft cheeks. In return, Ahni cooed and gurgled her love for them. She punched the air with her tiny fists before putting them into her mouth. Her little feet constantly kicked off her covers. Grammy oohed and aahed counting chubby fingers and toes as she blanketed the little girl.

By the time Pap arrived home from cutting wood the next day, Ahni was nursing while Grammy sang a lullaby from the old country. *Pium paum. The cradle rocks for the innocent child . . . Pium paum.* Little Ahni reached for Pap's thumb; gripped it in her little fist and brought it to her mouth. Pap felt his heart soften.

As Ahni grew strong and lively, Pap would pat her on the head as he brought fresh fish for the table. Grammy, too, forgot about the clouds that had hidden the sun during Ahni's birth. She held Ahni close as she told her stories every day. Stories from books. Stories about magical beings. Stories from the old country—the place she had come from as a newly-wed. She told how she and her husband had bought steerage tickets on a great ship that sailed the wide ocean to a new land where they could begin their life together.

Grammy whispered, "I carried your mother all the way across the ocean inside my own swollen belly." Grammy also whispered how the ship rocked and heaved, and the timbers creaked during a blustery storm. She whispered about the sickness that made Grammy run to the rail of the ship to spew everything she'd eaten into the waves pummeling the ship. Her husband had held her at the rail so *Iku* the fearsome monster of the waters wouldn't pull her into the foaming ocean to be his bride.

She whispered to Ahni, "Maybe that's why your mam was born without a voice to speak. Maybe my precious baby's voice was swept away in the swelling of the great waters below the ship. Or maybe *Iku*—slimy sea monster that he is—stole Mam's voice because the ship disturbed his sleep. Or maybe the water gods, the earth gods, and the sky gods all convened and agreed to punish me and my husband for the sin of lying together before the holy man united us. Their terrible punishment was to burden our unborn child by twisting her tongue so that she would never be able to untangle it to say a word."

Whatever the reason, Ahni's Mam had never been able to speak. Grammy's eyes filled with tears as she finished whispering in Ahni's ear. Ahni herself felt hollow and sad as she looked at her mother silently skinning a rabbit for the supper pot.

Grammy even told scary stories that frightened Ahni so much that she clung to the safety of Grammy's arms. Ahni shivered as Grammy told of the hungry and clawing monstrosity that lurked in the frozen and wintery wilds. Grammy shivered as she whispered, "Each time I say the name *Nalka*, I fear it will think I'm calling for it. I never say it aloud."

Ahni snuggled even closer to Grammy and tried to image the horrible creature that, instead of sating itself, grew hungrier each time it gorged on human flesh. She imagined the monster's skin wrinkled and scaly. He'd have squat legs and eyes that glowed green in the dark. His long sticky tongue snaked out to capture little girls in flash.

The day that Ahni turned three, her whole family rejoiced because she no longer wet the rags Mam and Grammy wrapped around her bottom. She no longer sucked her thumb, and holding Mam's hand, she could walk the whole way to the dry goods store without stumbling. Pap, too, was ever so pleased that she could talk—and talk she did—incessantly, but no one ever shushed her or told her it was time to let someone else talk. On the morning of her birthday, they celebrated with fried oat cakes dotted with raisins and sweetened with molasses.

Ever since Ahni had been able to walk, she followed Pap into the stable to watch him get ready for his day cutting wood. Her favorite thing was when Pap boosted her onto the broad back of Big Thunder and let her sit there stroking the horse's mane while he checked all the reins that hitched Big Thunder to the sledge.

Then Pap spent the day in the woods chopping tall trees. He loved working in the lush forest. He savored the delicate smell of the mosses he lay in to rest a bit after eating his noon sandwich. He sang as he chopped. He sang as he sawed. After he limbed trees and cut them into logs the right length for fireplaces and barrel stoves, he piled them onto his sledge. He then *giddi-up*-ed his stocky muscled horse toward home. After selling the logs, he spread the coins on the plank counter of the nearby trading post to buy slabs of bacon, smoked sausages, dried beans, oats, coffee, raisins, molasses, and a handful of hard candies for Ahni, he headed for home. There he was greeted with smiles, hugs, excitement, and the welcome aroma of toasting venison.

That was all before everything changed. Before the darkness came. Not an eclipse darkness, but a worse darkness.

One morning, when Ahni and Pap creaked open the stable door, Big Thunder didn't huff and stamp his hooves impatiently. Even the stable cat ran out the door instead of rubbing against Ahni's legs begging for warm milk.

Big Thunder was dead!

Pap pulled at his hair and moaned out loud. Ahni sprawled on the horse's broad belly, stroking him, whispering in his ear, and letting her tears fall onto his mane. "Git up, Big Thunder. Be strong. Not die an' leave me. I be lost without you."

Pap blew his nose in a blue rag, then wiped his eyes. "It was only time," he said as he shook Ahni by the shoulders. "It took this long, but the curse of darkness now shows itself. You and your eclipse birth caused Big Thunder to die. You're to blame! Born bad! I knew we should've left you in the forest for the wolves."

Frightened, Ahni broke away from Pap's grip and ran into the house with tear-stained cheeks. "Big Thunder dead! Pap say I born bad an' make him die!"

Mam and Grammy held her, rocked her. Her mother kissed her on the forehead, smoothed and braided her hair, calming her. Then she wrote the letters she'd been teaching Ahni on her hand. I-l-o-v-e-y-o-u. Ahni hugged her mother tightly, but her tears still threatened to fall.

"You're not born bad. You're my sweet Lamb-i-kins," Grammy said calming Ahni. "I'll tell you a story."

"Tell horse story. Horse good as Big Thunder." Ahni begged while Mam stirred an extra spoonful of brown sugar into Ahni's bowl of oat cereal.

Ahni snuggled next to Grammy, comforted by the wafting scent of cedar smoke. Grammy patted her chubby knees, called her *Dear, Sweet Lamb-i-kins*, and started her story.

"Once upon a time there was a beautiful horse named Pegasus. He was all white from the tips of his ears to his very hooves. Everyone loved Pegasus because he was good and kind. He even let smaller, shorter-legged horses win races. If someone needed a load of firewood pulled in a wagon, they could depend on Pegasus. He was so gentle, even the smallest of children could ride on his back without their mothers and fathers worrying that Pegasus would run like the wind tumbling them off."

Ahni forgot that she didn't suck her thumb anymore and stuck it into her mouth. She pictured a great white horse that was as strong and kind as Big Thunder.

"Unfortunately, a long drought fell upon the village. No rain fell; the river and all the wells dried up. Everyone was very thirsty. Even Pegasus. Just when everyone thought they'd die of thirst, Pegasus pawed the ground. One, two, three times. Nothing happened. He pawed again. Four, five, six. Nothing. Seven, eight. On the ninth, water erupted from the earth. A gushing fountain of cool, clean water burst into the air and flowed onto the thirsty ground! Everybody surrounded Pegasus calling him a hero and brought him armloads of clover and tall grasses. Children stroked Pegasus' white mane, braided daisies and dandelions into long chains and hung them around his neck.

"That made some of the other horses jealous. They plotted to kick him with their hooves scarring and making him ugly. That night they did. They struck his legs so much that that Pegasus became lame. He couldn't run races anymore, or carry loads of wood, or give children rides on his back.

"The town's people wailed and cried in distress. They begged their gods to heal Pegasus. He himself wished he could fly because his legs were useless. The sky gods agreed. Pegasus was such a good and gentle horse, they gave him wings. They invited him to fly to the stars and become one with them. He did so his people could then look up, see him in the heavens, and remember him forever and ever."

"That story happy, then sad, then happy again," Ahni said when Grammy ended. "Now that Big Thunder dead, will he go to sky an' can we see him ever night?"

"Because Big Thunder was a good and gentle hard worker, you can be sure his spirit will fly to the sky just like Pegasus' did. Tonight, when it's dark and the stars twinkle, you and I will go out to see the stars that are Pegasus. We'll tell Big Thunder's spirit to go there so we'll always remember him when we look to the stars."

Ahni was so excited to see the flying horse in the stars that she almost forgot to be sad about Big Thunder. Almost.

Ahni was not the only one lost without Big Thunder. Pap no longer went into the woods. He no longer returned smelling of pine and fresh air. Where he did go, Ahni didn't know, but she didn't like how he smelled when he returned. Neither did Mam or Grammy. Pap's breath was foul and disgusting. His eyes—red. His mood—wild and brutal. Ahni hid behind Mam when she heard his heavy tread on the path to their log hovel. She feared his blazing eyes that reminded her that she was eclipse-born. Born bad!

Ahni was eight years old when Pap pulled her by the ear and led her out into the rocky path that ran from their hut to the nearby settlement that grew a little every year. Ahni yowled!

"Time for ye to earn yer own way. I can't be feeding ye, yer mother, and old Grammy."

When they got home that night, no venison was roasting in the oven. The house was cold. Ahni shivered as she told Mam and Grammy, "I scared. Not know how to get anything, have no coins to give the store man for even a bit of moldy cheese. Pap show me how to grab an' hide what I take but not pay. I cried an' said, 'No. Not nice.'"

"He yank my arm 'most outta my shoulder yellin', 'Ye'll feel the strap on yer bare hinder if ye don't.'"

Grammy took Ahni into her arms and called her *Dear Sweet Lamb-i-kins*. She made Ahni feel a bit better, but she knew the next day would be the same. Pap would make her pick pockets, steal, or dig carrots and rutabagas from other people's gardens.

The next day, Ahni came home with a scabby rutabaga she'd found tossed aside near the path, Mam boiled the rutabaga then mixed it with some bacon grease. All the while, she wiped her eyes on the corner of her ragged apron. Pap didn't come home until long after Ahni and Grammy had unrolled their thin mattress onto the kitchen floor and pulled a worn quilt over themselves for the night. Pap roared asking what Ahni had brought home. Grammy hurried to fill a bowl with the mashed rutabaga. "What else?" he snarled.

Ahni showed him the soiled handkerchief she'd picked from a man's pocket. Pap pulled off his belt and swung hard.

Ahni whimpered, "I no good," as Grammy pulled her out of the way.

"That's for sure. Do I have to do everything myself while you three sit around all day telling stories?" Pap stumbled as he swung his belt again. Mam stepped in to save Ahni and the belt slashed against her legs. Grammy pulled the two of them outside where they shivered until they heard Pap snoring.

The next day, Grammy stood between Ahni and Pap refusing to let him take her. "I'll go to the fur trader's house and ask to wash their clothes or scrub their floors. I'll even scour their chamber pots. I'll do anything so Ahni doesn't have to go out stealing and getting beaten." She stared at Pap. "And you. There are plenty of jobs at logging camps that need workers. Or, you could hunt and fish if you'd just quit drowning your sorrows in the saloon."

Pap pushed Grammy aside so hard she fell against the wall. "I not be going out begging work from any other man. Live in one of their flea-ridden camps? Eat their sawdust bread and flat cakes? Not me! I only work for meself." Spittle flew from Pap's lips as he shouted the last words.

Mam sat quietly in the corner by the fireplace mending Pap's tattered overalls while Grammy and Pap argued back and forth. "You!" Pap said pointing to Mam. "You can help cook at one of the camps. You don't even need to talk. Maybe even better that you don't. Just follow orders. No sass. They's always be needing help stirring, mashing, and serving up that slop they call food, and scouring the big kettles and griddles. I'll take you and see to it that they treat you good. That's right. You women can work and not be expecting me to do ever thing."

Grammy stood, hands on hips. "And just what will you do all day when we're out scrubbing, mopping, and scouring for some meager food? Why aren't you out there snaring a rabbit or fishing for pike or tracking a deer?"

Pap stormed out the door. Grammy wrapped her thin shawl around her bony shoulders. "I'll go to ask the fur trader's wife for a scrubbing job. Ahni, you stay with Mam. If Pap comes home all liquored up, stay out of his way."

Mam and Ahni spent the day huddled by the fireplace. Ahni hummed while they played games like Guess Which Hand is Hiding the Pebble. After they tired of that, Mam drew letters on Ahni's hand, and Ahni said the word. *T-r-e-e. C-a-t. H-o-r-s-e. W-o-o-d.*

That reminded Ahni to put another log on the fire that had almost died out. The stack of wood was only two layers high. Ahni worried what would happen when it was all gone. Would Pap go out to the woods again to get more? Even without Big Thunder? Or would they freeze?

Grammy came home late. Pap and Mam were already on their corn-stalk and straw mattress in the other room. Pap snored wrapped in their only blanket. Mam shivered alongside him.

"Did you gots a job with fur trader's wife?" Ahni asked as Grammy groaned almost falling onto their bed. Ahni handed her the crust of bread she'd saved from their meager supper.

"Oh, you're such a good girl. Always thinking of your poor Grammy, but you eat it. I had something earlier."

"At fur trader's house?"

"No. They already have a cook and a woman who does the cleaning—even their windows were as shiny as the moon above, and you couldn't find a speck of dust anywhere in that big house if your life depended on it. They also have somebody who washes their clothes every week. Can you imagine? They didn't need me, but told me I should try the saloon down the way because their woman just caught a fever and died."

"A saloon? Like where Pap go gettin' drink that make him mean?"

"The same, but I don't pour the beer and such. I just mop up spills or scrub floors. When I'm not doing that, I stir a big pot of stew and keep adding chopped onion and rutabagas. Some of the bachelor men pay for a bowl or two because they have no one to cook for them at home. The saloon keeper let me eat a bowl for my work. Don't ask what kind of meat he put in it, but when Pap came in, the saloon man didn't ask him for money to pay for his drink. He just wrote something on a slip of paper."

Ahni thought about that. "You think Pap sold dead Big Thunder for saloon stew pot?"

"I don't know, but we haven't seen anything of Big Thunder cooking in our pot."

"You work hard? For jist a bowl of stew? Pap wants coins that jingle in pocket. He no like it."

Grammy pulled Ahni close to her. "Don't you worry now. I'll figure something out. Close your eyes and try to sleep."

CHAPTER 3

The next morning after Grammy set out to work at the saloon, Pap stuffed Mam and Ahni's few clothes into a burlap sack. Mam flew at him flailing her arms. Her eyes flamed with anger. Ahni was so frightened she tore the sack from Pap's hands yelling, "What you do? What goin' on?"

Pap pushed her away. "It's time for youse to work. No more lallygagging, burning up firewood, and telling stories all day. All three of you. Good for nothing. And you—born bad! Time to be productive. Do something for yourselves."

Mam tore at Pap again. Her lips and mouth stretched wide. Ahni could only imagine the screams that her mother would have been crying out, if she had been able. Ahni screeched as loud as she could. For herself. For Mam. She cried. She said all the bad words she had heard Pap say and ended with, "Stop hurting Mam, you wormy-faced fart!"

At that, Pap yelled, "I'll teach you. Calling me names!" He swung at Ahni, but she ducked under his arm. His powerful fist landed on Mam. Ahni ran out the door. He yelled after her, "Git back here afore I really hurt this feeble cow ye call yer Mam."

Ahni ran back in and stood between her Mam and Pap. Mam wiped her bleeding nose on her sleeve while she stroked Ahni's hair, then bent to pick up the sack of their clothes. Her eyes begged Ahni not to say another word. Ahni's eyes held her Mam as she said, "I sorry. I so sorry."

No more was said as Pap led them out of the house, down the lane, past the saloon, and toward the big woods where the logging camps were.

Winter was just beginning, but the cold chilled Ahni to the bone. Her fingers and toes tingled as she trudged along trailing Mam and Pap. The first night they slept in a farmer's barn covered with musty hay, but at least Ahni quit shivering when an orange stripped barn cat crawled under the hay and stretched next to her. The second night they huddled together under branches of a large pine. On the third day, they came to rough log buildings alongside a river. Pap went into one and came out with a broad-shouldered man with a black beard and mustache covering most of his face.

The man spit a dark brown glob into the freshly fallen snow as he looked Ahni and Mam up and down. "They good workers? Know anything about cookin' and cleanin'?" the man asked wiping his mouth on his sleeve.

"Best here arounds," Pap replied smiling broadly.

"That little one thar . . . looks too small for much."

"She ken sweep and scrub and carry things. Not eat much. Never complaining. Never sassing. If she does, jist give her the belt across the hinder." Pap squeezed Ahni's shoulder.

Ahni winced and shook his hand off, scowling. This was a logging camp, and Pap was leaving them way out in the woods. He was happy about it. He'd probably go back and sit in the saloon drinking up the whole worth of Big Thunder's meat while he got himself crazy drunk. She and Mam would be stuck here working themselves weary, but maybe they'd be fed, like the saloon man let Grammy have a bowl of Big Thunder stew every day she worked.

"Well," the man said. "We can't be fussy. As long as they work, and work hard, we can use them in the cook shack."

Pap left. He turned his back and walked away as fast as he could into the falling snow. Ahni watched the big man with the black beard open a pouch of chew tobacco and pinch out a bit that he put between his cheek and teeth. Then he said, "Follow me. Name's Axel. I'll show ye around and get you working. O'er there's the bunkhouse for the loggers. Stay out of it. Stables for horses—straight ahead. There's the shit shack that way. The cook shack and mess hall in that building there. Go tell the cook you're ready to work."

He turned away, but Ahni asked, "Where we sleep?"

"Thinking of sleeping and you haven't even done one stitch of work yet?"

Mam pulled Ahni close and rushed her into the cook shack. Ahni's eyes filled with tears. She hated Pap for bringing them to the camp way out in the big forest far from home and Grammy. Two men and a woman were in the cook shack. The woman wore a scarf wound around her head. She kneaded a huge batch of dough on a table made of planks. One man with a scar over one eye brow chopped at joints of meat with a heavy cleaver. The other frowned as he pealed a pile of potatoes and rutabagas that was so high, Ahni almost couldn't see the man behind it.

"We here to work," Ahni tried to say, but her throat felt stiff and frozen so the words came out more like *ee-eer t'erk*. She cleared her throat. All three looked up. She said again, "We here to work."

"Well, glory be." The woman pounded the dough with her fists. "Finally, some help. Axel's been promising for days. Harry, what do you want them to do first?"

The tall skinny man with the scar stopped chopping meat into chunks and looked them over. "What's your names?" he asked taking a swipe at his nose with his sleeve.

"Mam no talk, but she work good an' understand words. Jist point an' tell an' she do."

"Does she have a name other than Mam?"

Ahni had never heard her mother called anything but Mam, so she shrugged and looked at her mother. Mam nodded. Ahni held out her hand. Mam drew letters on her hand. *F-l-o-r-a.*

"Her name Flora. Mine Ahni."

"Well, Flora and Ahni. There's plenty to do here. Set your sack over there in the corner. Flora, help with pealing that pile of potatoes and rutabagas."

The woman stopped kneading the dough. A drop of sweat dripped off her chin and fell into the bowl as she said, "I'm Eleanor. Call me Ellie. That there," she pointed to the meat chopper, "is Harry. And the grumpy potato peeler is Alfred. Now we know each other. Let's get busy. Come dark the woodsmen will all be stomping in hungrier than bears just out of hibernation and looking for their food."

Harry wiped his hands on his bloody apron. "How old are you, Ahni?"

"Eight, I think." She held up eight fingers. "I big enough to do lots, but not chop at big pile of meat." Ahni looked at what she hoped had not been a good horse like Big Thunder.

Harry signaled Ahni to follow him. He pointed to a corner that was heaped with piles of rags, brooms, mops, and buckets. "Know how to use these things?" he asked looking at her skinny arms and legs.

"They for sweep, scrub, clean," Ahni said, glad that she knew. She thought of Grammy who would be scrubbing and stirring pots of stew at the saloon at that moment. Ahni knew she could do it here, too. Besides, she could smell good things cooking on the big stove. She hoped she wouldn't be going to bed hungry that night.

"Good. You'll be our mess hall girl. Before meals, get plates, mugs, knives, forks, spoons, bowl—whatever we'll need for the meal. Get them all stacked and ready on the tables. When the men get here, carry out platters and bowls of food. You gotta be fast about it, but not so fast you drop or spill. They're hungry and tired after a whole day in the woods. After meals, bring dirty dishes to the kitchen, clean tables, sweep and scrub the floor. We run a clean mess in this camp. Mr. Big Owner doesn't want any loggers getting sick and leaving."

"How I know when to get ready for eating time?" Ahni looked at the two long tables with benches on either side.

"You need to be ready way before the sun rises in the morning. The loggers need to eat plenty and drink a lot of hot coffee before they head to the woods. They begin work when it's barely daylight in the swamp. Then they work all day and are back here just after sun-down. They eat their noon meal in the woods so you don't have to worry about setting tables for that. Still, you'll be plenty busy. Probably even help peeling potatoes and such when you're done cleaning in the morning."

Ahni wanted to ask where she and Mam would be sleeping. She hoped it would be somewhere warm, but Harry had thrust a broom into her hands and turned back to the plank where he was butchering the meat.

Ahni's empty stomach clawed for food. Sweeping and scrubbing made her even hungrier. Her arms and legs ached. She didn't think she could even sweep one more cob web or peel one more rutabaga when she heard horses pulling a sledge through the crusty snow.

"Bowls and plates all stacked on the tables?" Harry asked. "Spoons and mugs, too?"

Harry yelled directions to everyone. "Get the bread on the tables, now. Pret' soon we hear boots on the floor. Then it's time to run the hot stew out." Mam scooped stew into kettles for Ahni to run to the tables. Ellie pulled bread pudding out of the big oven. Alfred handed Ahni a coffee pot so big and heavy she almost dropped it.

Run! Run! Run! Ahni's legs ached as she ran with platters of bread. Kettles of stew. More bread. More steaming pots of coffee. More bread pudding. More and more everything. The loggers didn't say a word as they ate. The only noises were the clanking of spoons cleaning the last bits of meat from tin bowls. The loggers hadn't even taken their jackets off when they sat at the tables, but they'd all taken off their hats and set them on their knees.

When the men finished and went to their bunk house for the night, Ahni let out a big sigh of relief until she realized that her job for the night had just begun. She already felt like she could drop right where she was and not wake up for two days. And she still hadn't eaten anything.

When she carried the first load of stacked bowls into the kitchen, Harry said, "Let's eat our supper before we clean all this up and get ready for the morning rush."

Ahni didn't know if she should be happy that she was finally getting to eat, or sad that there was so much yet to be done before she got to lie down. She still wondered where she and Mam would sleep for the night, but didn't dare ask. Could she even make it through the clean-up before falling asleep on her feet? And then face another day?

CHAPTER 4

Ahni awoke to a heavy clomping of boots and the clanging of pots. It took her a while to fight her way up through the thick fog of sleep to realize where she was. She and Mam huddled under the one ragged blanket Pap had stuffed into the burlap sack for them. They slept on the floor to the side of the big cook stove. It had been warm enough, and Ahni's hunger had been soothed by bowls of meaty stew and warm slabs of bread pudding that Ellie made the night before. Food and a warm place to sleep—Ahni smiled thinking about them until she tried to turn over. Every part of her body cried with an aching torture she'd never known before.

Harry called, "Get up. No time for lie-abouts. As they say to the horses, *giddy-up.*"

Ellie bent over Mam and Ahni whispering, "I know you're hurting all over from the work, but you'll get used to it. I cried my first three days here. The work is not so hard as it is constant."

Ahni knew that. Every ache told her. Ellie continued, "You'll be busy every day, every minute of every long day. For me, my only relief comes when all the work is done. Then I get to go to the stables where Tarmo, my husband, takes care of the horses when they aren't pulling the log sledges from the woods to the river."

The word horses got Ahni attention. The night before, Ellie had smelled like baked bread and cinnamon from the pudding when she'd showed Mam and Ahni where to spread their blanket for the night. Now Ellie smelled like the straw that had filled Big Thunder's stable. She smelled like Big Thunder had smelled, too.

It was still dark out. Ahni wrapped herself in the ragged blanket to head to the biffy before starting her day. Her legs ached. Her shoulders and arms, too. A furrow of boot prints formed a path from outhouse to the logger's bunk house. Before she even got to the door, Ahni heard laughter coming from the outhouse. Then the door burst open. A logger stumbled out. In the dim moon light, Ahni saw him still pulling up his pants and yanking a suspender over his shoulder.

"Well, lookie here, guys. The new gal from the cook shack is here wanting company."

Loud guffaws echoed from inside the out-house. Ahni knew from the night before that there were five holes on the long bench inside, and now it sounded like they all had a logger sitting on them. Her heart pounded. Her bowels were urging her. They needed emptying, but she could not force herself to take a step further.

"C'mon in, missy. There's a hole just waiting for you. Kinda smelly in here, but nice and warm." More hooting and laughter bounced off the walls.

Ahni shivered in fear more than the cold. Her tired legs froze in place, but she needed to go. Go to the biffy and get back to the kitchen. Tarmo came up behind her and said, "You're not really wanting to go in there right now. How abouts I walk you back to the kitchen. Ask my wife Ellie. She'll probably let you use her chamber pot."

"T-thanks. I find my way. I ask Ellie." With that Ahni retraced her steps to the kitchen.

Harry growled at Ahni when she returned from the stables where Ellie had sent her to use her chamber pot that was really just a pail with a narrow board laid across to sit on. "Can't waste good morning time running about. Get those plates and things on the tables, then come back here to help sizzle sausages."

Mam was already mixing something in a giant bowl. Ellie measured out salt and flour. Alfred poured maple syrup into pitchers, then he stoked up the fire in the huge stove and put a long cast iron griddle on top. Next, he scooped lard with his hands and spread it on the griddle.

"Get that flap jack batter mixed and ready. It won't be long before they all come stomping in here."

Ellie took over mixing the batter so Mam could help Harry make piles of sand-wiches for the men to take into the woods for their noon meal.

Alfred handed Ahni a long fork and pointed to the sausages. "Sizzle 'em good, but don't let them burn or Harry'll have yer hide."

After breakfast, Ahni and Alfred set huge platters of sausage sandwiches at the end of each table. The men grabbed three each and jammed them into their coat pockets before heading outside.

When Ahni was done cleaning tables and sweeping, Harry told her to help in the kitchen until time to set up for night meal. "Alfred, when you're done with the dishes, get the mop out and scrub the mess hall."

Alfred fussed, "Bad enough I have to wash dishes. I didn't hire on to be no mess hall girl."

Harry reminded him that there were other camps that might like a complainer and not feed him as well, so Alfred took the mop and scrub buckets without saying another word. Harry continued calling out what was needed as he poured bags of dried beans into huge kettles.

"Ellie, get started on the bread. We'll need at least thirty loaves for tomorrow's sandwiches. Flora, you know how to make pie crust?"

Mam nodded.

"Good. Lard's in them pails in the back room. Get flour there, too. Start on the crusts. We need to get the pies baked—eight of 'em—before the breads are ready for the oven."

"Ahni, go with your mother. Bushels of apples are in the back room, too. If you need more, they're out in the storage shed. I'll go with you to the storage shed. We'll bring in the hams, potatoes, carrots, and rutabagas so Alfred can start peeling potatoes when he'd done slopping up the mess hall. And you finish with the apples."

After helping Harry lug in all the root vegetables from storage, Ahni filled pails of cold water from outdoor pump. The wind whipped at her hair, pulling it out of the sloppy braid she'd hurriedly plaited it into that morning. She shivered in her thin dress, wishing she had taken the ragged blanket to wrap around herself.

Harry helped carry the pails inside to heat on the big stoves for washing dishes and for the bean soup. He noticed Ahni shivering. "You need more than those clothes if you're going to help at all outside. Ask Ellie if she has a sweater or shawl you can borrow." Ahni was surprised that Harry cared about her comfort. Pap wouldn't even have noticed how cold she was.

After all the pumping and carrying, Ahni rubbed her cold and tired arms. The day was just beginning. When she started peeling apples, Harry asked if she'd eaten yet.

"No time. Busy alla time," she answered.

"We all need to eat now." There weren't any sausages left from the logger's meal, so Harry cut chunks of ham for everyone and they made sandwiches from the left-over ends of bread. Ahni couldn't remember when she'd had such a thick slab of juicy meat. She ate quickly, licked her fingers, then got to work peeling. She wanted Harry to notice that she wasn't one to lollygag, and that she earned her ham sandwiches and bowls of stew.

CHAPTER 5

Snow piled up as the day went on. At noon, Ahni and the rest of the kitchen crew took a few minutes to sit with bowls of stew left over from the day before. Harry said, "We still need one more helper to pump water and get all the meals ready on time. Flora and Ahni have made a big difference, but if we don't get more than a minute to grab a bite to eat or go to biffy, we're going to wear ourselves out until we're no better than limp dish rags."

Alfred stuffed another spoonful into his mouth. "Yeah. Get some big strong guy who can mop and scrub. I don't mind being up to my elbows in the dish water, but pushing that mop is more than I care to do. And there otta be a law again spitting tobakky on floors. The spitters should clean up their own messes."

"I know what you mean, but Axel wouldn't say a word to them because he chews and spits wherever he wants. We'll get no help from him. It's a filthy habit, that's for sure."

Ellie stirred another spoonful of brown sugar into her coffee. "Mr. Woods, or the *Big Boss Man* as you all call him, seldom comes around, but he's fussy about how everything is run, maybe he'd say we could fine the tobacco spitters or something."

"He'd have my hide and fire me if I didn't run a clean kitchen with lots of good food, so you'd think he'd care about something like that." Harry rubbed his neck. "All I hear from Mr. Woods is that he expects good and plenty food to keep the crews happy and not jumping off to work at some other camp where they might get fed better."

"But first, we need an extra person here. Maybe Axel can get Mr. Woods to hire someone on. He could pump and bring in water, too. We'd have no trouble keeping him busy from daybreak to sundown. Earlier and later, too." Ellie poured a bit more coffee for herself, then offered the pot to Mam.

Ahni listened. She doubted if Pap would ever come to the camp to scrub floors. He'd been so proud of Big Thunder and the work he did all by himself in the forest, cutting, and selling wood so he'd have money to buy things like a smoked ham, sacks of flour and oats, molasses and even a new dress or shoes when Mam or Grammy needed them. Here was a job with lots of food and a warm place to sleep, but he probably would never do it.

Harry clanked his spoon against his empty tin bowl and said, "Well, we don't have that extra person, so let's get busy."

It was only her second day at the camp, but Ahni had already figured out the best way to do her job. There was a small table in one corner of the hall where Axel who was the camp boss sat with Reino, the woods boss. Reino was bow-legged with bushy white eyebrows and beard. He hardly spoke to anyone in the cook shack—just came in to eat and left again. Ellie had whispered to Ahni that she should always bring food to the two bosses, Axel and Reino, at the little table first. "My husband Tarmo who takes care of the horses sits there with them sometimes, too."

In the middle of the dining area was a great round wood heater. Harry and Alfred always made sure it was loaded with wood, and that the fire roared before the men came from the woods so the hall would be as warm as it could be during the cold winter. On either side of the wood heater was a long table. Ten loggers sat at one, eleven at the other.

As she carried pails of the ham and bean soup to the tables, Ahni listened to the men say the few words they said before ducking their heads to eat. Some spoke English most of the time. Yet she heard more than one other language as she set food on the tables. Ahni had no idea what the other languages were, but one of them sounded like words that her Grammy had spoken to Mam sometimes. She wished she knew what country Grammy had come from. She liked bringing coffee and full bowls of food to that table. The men always nodded thanks to her.

Also seated at that table were the loggers who were often jostled and teased by some of the others. Ahni heard them called *Injuns* more than once. Her Grammy had told her never to use that word. "They're Ojibwe. Good people. They and their families and their long-ago grandmas and grandpas have been in this land way before any settlers came from across the ocean and pushed them off their land." Ahni liked those men. They never tried to grab or poke her when she brought the food. They, too, nodded thanks.

When Ahni brought out the apple pies, Alfred followed carrying full pots of coffee. The men whistled their appreciation when they saw the pie. Mam peered around the corner to watch if the men liked her pies. With a few chews and swallows, their tin plates emptied of the huge slice of pie in no time.

When the wind gusted shaking the wood framed hall, one of the men stood, "Looks like the Wiindigoo is out looking for warm flesh tonight." Some men hooted and laughed as they got up to leave, too. "Wiindigoo, Wiindigoo. Catch me if you can."

Ahni was stacking plates at the Ojibwe table. She noticed that none of those loggers laughed. "What's the *Wiindigoo*?" she asked not knowing if they'd understand her.

"Wiindigoo is nothing to laugh at," a man who appeared to be quite young answered.

Another joined in, "Wiindigoo is monster who whirls in with winter winds. He is human-flesh eating monster. Some say he is hunter who got lost in the forest and was bitten by evil. Now he's evil as can be. Always wanting more. And more. Never satisfied."

One of the older Ojibwe loggers nodded and said softly, "Just like some men I know."

Ahni wondered about what she heard. Grammy had told her about invaders who'd come to her home country. They'd taken the best farms as their own, the best forests for hunting, the best lakes and rivers for fishing. Grammy had said they were like *Nalka*, the repulsive monster of their folklore who trampled fields killing the crops, and then they drank whole lakes drying up the surrounding lands. Grammy's story had been frightening. In his greed, *Nalka* left the farmers and villagers starving and suffering.

Wind rattled the three small windows in the hall and howled as the men finished the last bites of pie. Then they went to their bunks, told stories while sharpening their saws, smoking a pipe, or playing a game of cards before they blew out their candle lamps and went to sleep.

After all the loggers left, Alfred helped Ahni carry the first loads of dishes to the kitchen so he could start washing. On her second trip with an armload of soup bowls, Ellie called her over to the long plank table where she sliced bread for the next day's sandwiches. "Come and meet my husband. Tarmo, this here's Ahni our mess hall girl. And this is Flora, her mam."

Ahni liked Tarmo right away. He was the man who'd saved her at the outhouse her first night in the camp. He took the stack of bowls from her, picked her up, and swung her in a circle. "Looks like you've come to the right place. They'll feed you up good here and you'll get so much meat on your bones, you'll pop right out of that dress."

Ahni giggled. It felt good. She hadn't giggled for a long time. The best part of Tarmo was that he smelled like the horses he'd been feeding and watering since the woods crews had come in for the night. Memories of Big Thunder and his smell filled her eyes with tears. No wonder she liked Tarmo.

"Tarmo, quit your foolishness and eat your supper. Ahni, run him this bowl of soup along with some hard tack from the back room. Set it down on that little table where the bosses sit." Ellie said all that while she poured a mug of coffee for her husband and handed Ahni an extra slab of ham to put in his bowl.

Alfred was already up to his elbows in dishwater. "Hurry and bring me the coffee mugs and pie plates. I wanna get to sleep sometime tonight, too. And I suppose I gotta mop the floor yet, seeing as how you don't have any meat on your bones, as Tarmo would say."

Ellie and Harry started measuring flour for the morning's flapjacks. Flora carried baskets of apples from the store room to make a sauce.

Stacking dishes and running them to the kitchen didn't seem as hard as it had the night before because Tarmo and Ellie kept up a light-hearted banter the whole time. Ahni listened and smiled. Maybe at one time Mam and Pap had been the same way, but it was so long ago, she didn't remember.

"Want more soup, Lazy Bones?" Ellie called to Tarmo.

"Who you calling Lazy Bones? I happen to know you kitchen folk just sit around pulling taffy and telling stories all day."

"Huh! Look who's talking? I know you. Snoring up a storm in a pile of straw while the horses are out slaving in the woods. In fact, I think you snored so loud all day that you stirred up this storm!"

Ahni laughed as softly as she could while wiping spills from the tables. Tarmo noticed. "Hey, how abouts you quit that for now and have a bowl of this delicious soup that woman who calls herself my wife is going to scoop into a bowl for you and maybe sneak in an extra chunk of ham, too? Then I'll mop the floor while that sour puss Alfred takes an early night off so he can join the poker game going on in the bunk house."

"You mean that?" Alfred asked.

"Just this one time, but don't come crying to me when you lose all your money, your shirt and belt, too."

Alfred started whistling and washing the last dishes as fast as he could, then he headed out the door. "Thanks again," he called over his shoulder.

Tarmo laughed. "Good luck and don't let the Wiindigoo get you out there in the dark."

"Don't believe in that ridiculous tale," Alfred snickered. "Good night."

CHAPTER 6

The wind howled outside slapping tree branches against the wood walls of the dining hall. It was as eerie as could be. Ahni was glad to be inside with Mam, Tarmo, Ellie, and Harry as they all sat around the little corner table. Every bean and every lump of ham fat had been scraped from the soup pot. The pie plates looked like they'd been licked clean by the time they all sat back rubbing their tummies.

"That good food!" Ahni smiled as she stacked the last bowls.

"Flora and I'll wash those and get the kitchen all slicked up for tomorrow," Ellie said as Tarmo grabbed the mop to finish Alfred's job as promised. Ahni straightened benches at the tables and checked to make sure no crumbs or spills lurked on any of the tables.

The wind whipped snow against the little window. "What happen if storm get bigger an' bigger?" Ahni asked Tarmo.

"It's happened," he said resting against the mop. "In late March of the first year I joined a logging camp, we were all looking forward to spring. We wanted to see dandelions instead of snow banks. Robins instead of the *Wiindigoo*."

"What everyone do when big storm come?"

"That storm shut us all down. The snow was so deep, the horses couldn't get through. No horses meant no loggers could go out to the woods and chop. The wind blew so hard, it swirled snow for two days. We couldn't as much as see our way from bunkhouse to outhouse to mess hall to stables. That's when I began sleeping with the horses. They kept me warm, but I worried about running out of feed for them if the blizzard lasted too long."

"What you eat iffn you couldn't get to mess hall?"

"Me? In case you haven't noticed, I'm right smart at times. When I figured out that the storm was going to be a big blow, I grabbed me a sack and stuffed it with a whole ham, some hard tack, a handful of carrots, some rutabagas, onions, and apples."

Ahni was glad Tarmo had been so smart and said so.

"Smart, yes, but not smart enough to grab a knife. You ever try to eat a whole ham or rutabaga without a knife to cut and slice?"

"No, but if I had big hungers, I woulda tore 'em apart with me fingers an' teeth."

"Well, I had those, but I had something else, too. I not only feed and water the horses, but I have to take care of their hooves, too. A horse's feet and hooves are their most important parts after their stomachs. I didn't need a kitchen knife after all. I had my farrier tools. I had a rasp, nippers, hoof knives, and a hoof pick. Turns out, that's all I needed."

Ahni nodded. She remembered leaning against the stable wall as Pap lifted each of Big Thunder's feet each evening after they came in from the woods so he could inspect the hooves. "Lotsa horses here?"

"Eight. Two teams. And each horse has four legs. That's thirty-two hooves I check every night. Have to rasp rough spots. Cut, pick, and nip if needed." Tarmo stopped and winked at Ellie who was listening as she and Mam finished their work in the kitchen. He pointed to his wife and whispered to Ahni, "And she calls me Lazy Bones! Thirty-two hooves. You hear that, Ellie? Add 'em up. Thirty-two hooves every day!"

Harry burst out in a loud laugh. Then lowered his voice and looked around before saying, "Only lazy-bones in this whole camp is Axel. What does he do all day when the loggers are in the woods, and we're all slaving in the kitchen?"

Tarmo came to Axel's defense saying, "Well, he hunts and fishes with me to keep fresh meat on our table. He and I fix what needs fixing. Stove pipes, rattling windows and such. We shovel paths. Clean ashes and klinkers outta stoves. Carry wood and pump water." Tarmo stopped to wipe his nose on his sleeve.

"Besides all that, he keeps track of the supplies in the store room for the men and for the animals. He gets what we need. He makes sure we have enough oil and candles for our lanterns. And best of all, he knows about horses and how to keep them healthy. Without the horses, we shut down."

Ahni understood that. After Big Thunder died, Pap didn't work in the woods anymore.

Tarmo continued, "He even helps me check all the horse gear for wear. Every night when they come into the stable, he watches how they walk to make sure none are getting lame, or have sores that cause trouble."

Harry admitted, "Ya, he does lots to keep the camp running, and he keeps us well supplied, not like some camps I've heard that some run out of food from time to time and the men go hungry."

"Whatever else you say about Mr. Woods, he makes sure we have enough to eat. Now if he'd bring us one more mess hall worker, I'd be really happy," Harry chucked some more wood into the big kitchen stove. He said to Flora, "Don't be afraid to keep the stove stoked at night. We've got plenty of wood and don't want you and Ahni getting cold."

Flora smiled. Ahni thought how beautiful Mam was at that moment. It had been a long time since she'd seen her smile. They had plenty of food. A warm place to sleep. The days were long with lots of work, but she and Mam were in the company of good people who cared about them. Ahni felt content as she hung up her cleaning rags and watched as everyone finished their chores. Tarmo held Ellie's hand as they walked the length of the dining area snuffing out candle lanterns.

As Mam filled the big stove with wood for the night, Ahni thought about all the wood that Pap had brought out of the woods all by himself with only Big Thunder to help. He'd worked hard. For a short moment she wished Pap was there with them, but then she remembered his drunken rages and his refusal to find other work after Big Thunder died. She didn't think he'd fit in here at the camp. Not like Harry and Tarmo. She felt a bit guilty, but she was glad he wasn't with them.

CHAPTER 7

The wind calmed during the night, but large flakes fell softly muffling the sound of a pack of wolves howling in the distance. Ahni shivered as she heard the mournful howls. As the pack moved away, the chorus faded, but the eeriness remained.

That night Ahni awoke often hearing Mam moaning a bit in her sleep. At those times, she reached and gently laid her hand on her mother's shoulder hoping to calm her. It was so unusual to hear any sounds from Mam that she wondered what she could possibly be dreaming. Ahni's own dreams swirled disturbing her sleep. In one, Ellie, Tarmo, and Harry were wolves. They snapped at Alfred, baring their teeth when he tried to leave the kitchen without having peeled a mountain of potatoes. Then she dreamed about horses with eight legs each. Eight legs. Eight hooves. And that she was trying to pick ice from the hooves, but each bit of ice she got out, a bigger one grew.

Ahni awoke to hear Mam and Harry filling the huge fire chamber of the cook stove with chunks of wood. Harry was speaking softly. "Maybe we can get Axel to ask Mr. Woods to get a mattress, or at least a corn shuck pad for you and Ahni to sleep on. Even the horses have bedding that's not a hard floor."

Ahni wished Mam could talk and thank Harry for being so thoughtful. If they got better bedding, she would thank him. She pushed off the thin blanket and tried to force herself to get up. Her arm muscles still ached from carrying food bowls and wiping the long tables clean. Her legs felt like daggers pierced into them. Her neck and back complained as she tried to roll so she could stand and get ready for the day. Ellie had told her she'd get used to the constant work. She wondered how many days that would take.

When the loggers stomped in, cold air blew in by the open door. "Hurry and shut that door," Harry called out.

Snow drifted in, too. The men brushed snow from their shoulders and slapped their hats on their knees before they sat. "Cold as a witch's . . ." The man stopped and looked at Ahni. "Guess I have to watch my language now that we have the ears of a young one around here." He gave a slight bow to Ahni and said, "Pardon me my bad manners."

Ahni set a huge tin bowl of oatmeal at the end of the man's table. She smiled at the man not knowing what to say. She didn't know what he'd been about to say about the witch that could be so bad that it needed an apology. Before the men had come in, she and Mam had put bowls of raisins, molasses, butter, and dried apples on each table. In no time, the men were scooping them on top of the oatmeal they'd ladled into their bowls and were silently spooning it into their mouths.

Alfred brought out big buckets of coffee. The men filled their own coffee mugs by dipping them right into the bucket. Some justled to be among the first to scoop so they wouldn't get a mug half full of the coarse grind.

One of the men at the last table asked Ahni what her name was when she came there to see if they needed their oatmeal bowl refilled. "Ahni," she said, not sure if she should be talking to the man or not. There seemed to be so many rules she didn't know about.

"Mine's Kalle. What brings you so young to be working way out here in the woods?"

Another spoke up with a laugh. "Kalle, whose name should be *Peikko*. *Peikko*, the scary giant who kidnaps children who are lost in the woods. Ahni, don't go wandering in the woods, or big bad *Peikko* will kidnap you."

Ahni didn't think Kalle looked like a giant who'd kidnap anyone, so she said, "Mam's here with me. Pap brought us to work."

"You'd be better off kidnapped by the *Peikko* or even charmed by the forest goblins who lure children to go deeper into the forest until they are lost forever. Maybe then *Mielikki*, the forest goddess, would take you into her wooden castle and take care of you like she does for all the lost animals."

"Don't listen to my friends here. They're full of folktales and foolishness. They're good for telling around a warm fire, but not to a hardworking girl like you," said Kalle. "Enough for now, men, it's time to get to the woods before half the day is gone."

After the men left, Tarmo came in for his breakfast. "Did all the teams get off without a hitch?" asked Ellie.

"Yup, they did. Now I'm wanting a bowl of oatmeal with molasses and raisins if there's any left." He sat at the bosses' little table watching Ahni stack and carry a stack of tin bowls to the sink where Alfred was rolling up his sleeves. He called to Alfred, "Win or lose last night?"

"A little of both," Alfred answered. "I'm about even. Just a little down. We didn't play too long. Everyone needed to sharpen their saws before time to blow out the candles, so there wasn't much time to play."

Ahni hoped Ellie and Tarmo would tease each other like they had the night before, but Tarmo was eager to finish his breakfast. "Axel and I plan to go hunting today after we shovel the paths. I think we need to hang the ropes from building to building, too. I feel in my bones that we're in for a big blow one of these days."

"You and your bones," Ellie chided as she started stirring the dough for the day's bread. Harry spread green beans on flat trays and slid them into the ovens to roast. Ahni was curious what he was doing so she asked, "What kind them beans?"

"They're coffee beans. When we get sacks of them, they're green—not good for making coffee. I roast them until they're dried and brown. Then we'll all get our chance at grinding them in that there grinder." He pointed to a shelf. "It's tiresome work, but the men like coffee better than tea or plain water, so Mr. Woods insists we do it. Keeps the men happy. Keeps me happy, too. Trouble is, we only have half a sack left and logging season is just starting. If Axel can't find more when he takes a trip into town, we'll be drinking hot water with cedar boughs in it. The men will grumble. I will, too."

Ellie piped up, "Tomorrow is Saturday. Axel will probably head for Port Charlie for supplies."

Harry had finished with the coffee beans and was pouring peas into one of the huge pots. "Pea soup tonight," he said. "We'll need potatoes and carrots. Along with another ham." He said that last part to Mam. She headed to the storeroom at the back of the cook shack. Ahni rubbed her shoulders and wondered when the constant aching would be over.

"Not only Saturday," Alfred said loading the wooden draining rack with bowl, "but pay day!"

"And the next day is Sunday. A day off for the loggers, but not for the horse man," said Tarmo.

"At least you won't have to lift thirty-two hooves on Sunday," Ellie smiled at him.

"Yup, maybe I'll even have time for a roll in the hay," Tarmo smiled back at Ellie.

Harry laughed, "You, two! Quit flirting with each other and get busy. Tarmo, I think there's some paths that need shoveling. And Axel is probably already out tracking some deer that need to be hanging ready to be skinned and made into venison meat pies."

"Apple bread pudding for supper?" Ellie asked Harry. "Or apple raisin pudding?"

"We have lots of rice," Harry answered, "so make a rice pudding with raisins and apple."

CHAPTER 8

Sunday came. A light dusting of snow fell onto the logging camp during the night making everything look lightly sugared. No clouds kept the sun from shining on the new-fallen snow and sparkling like it was covered with tiny diamonds.

Breakfast was much later than usual so that the loggers could sleep in. Ahni and Mam and the rest of the kitchen crew slept until nature called for them to stir from their bedding and head for the outhouse. For Ahni and Mam that meant scuttling their way to the stables where Tarmo had set up a pail with a board across in a far corner. Mam, Ahni, and Ellie took turns pulling the deer skin across the corner to provide them with some privacy.

Harry and his helpers stirred up a big corn meal mush for breakfast. With molasses poured on top, it was a treat that everyone looked forward to. Ahni licked the sweetness from her lips and even suffered through another bowl of mush, just to get more molasses.

To Ahni's surprise, the loggers stacked and carried their own bowls and mugs to the kitchen for Alfred to wash. There was one Ojibwe logger who always smiled and thanked her at the end of meals. "Why you help?" she asked.

"Sunday, today," he answered. "No work in woods. Just good day to get bath, wash clothes, and hear reading from good book."

Like many of the loggers, he spoke enough English, but talked with others at the table in their own language. Ahni loved listening to him and the other Ojibwe because their language was beautiful. Theirs words flowed together like a song, and their voices were soft and kind.

When the kitchen and the mess area were clean, Harry said, "Easy meals today." We all deserve as much rest time as we can get. Tarmo and Axel already skinned the deer they got, so let's get it roasting over a pit fire. We'll have enough venison for the whole day and then some leftover for a stew some other day."

The buck had been hanging behind the bunk house. A rope wove around the base of its antlers so the whole carcass hung from a thick branch lashed to two trees. Ahni watched in amazement as two men carefully cut it down and carried it to the fire pit.

While some loggers set the carcass to be roasted, others brought wood into a teepee-like structure. Another group did the same, but they piled wood into a round, domed structure made of bent saplings then covered with cedar boughs and deer hide. A deer skin hung over the opening of each to keep the heat in.

Ahni was as curious as could be about the little structures. "What they for?"

"Baths! Steam baths! Saunas!" a ruddy faced logger answered. "We're all itching to have a bath. And that's for real. We are itching! Time to steam the bugs out of our clothes and our hair." He mimicked scratching all over his body and hair. Ahni laughed as he danced a hop, skip, and jump while scratching.

While the men piled more wood outside the structures, they argued back and forth about which made a better steam bath, Ojibwe tepee, or the Finn's sauna dome.

"The same to me," said Harry. Once you get the wood burning, throw a little water on the hot rocks, the steam gets you sweating all the dirt off you real good."

The men finished by spreading freshly cut cedar boughs in a thick blanket on the ground around the stone fire ring. Everywhere Ahni looked the loggers were busy. They built wooden frames over the fires and hung big tubs filled with water to heat.

Harry explained, "Besides taking baths on Sundays, everyone washes clothes while the venison is roasting. Everyone'll eat their fill before the sun sets."

"Sound like good day." Ahni said.

"Yup, it will be. And I saved a special treat for you, your Mam, and the rest of the cook shack crew."

"What be it?"

"Secret. But when the loggers are full of venison, hanging their clothes to dry in the bunk house, playing cards, wrestling, and who knows all what else, we'll go back to the kitchen to bake bread for tomorrow, you'll find out what the surprise is then."

Ahni ran to find Mam to tell her that there'd be a special treat that night. She found her mother with Ellie looking in the tepee-shaped steam bath that was heating up and getting ready for the first bathers.

"After sun set, Harry have big surprise for us!"

Mam smiled and slid her hand around Ahni's shoulders. Even in the chilly air, she felt warm. Today, she'd have her first steam bath ever. Her one extra dress would get washed. Ellie and Tarmo were good people. Harry was kind and had a special treat ready for them. She couldn't wait to find out what it was.

When it was their turn, Ahni and Mam waited while Tarmo set a bucket of warm water inside the little fir and cedar branch-covered steam dome that he called a *sauna*. He explained that if they poured a little water on the hot rocks, steam would fill the inside and warm them to a nice cleansing sweat. They could use water from the bucket to wash themselves. Mam lifted the deer hide, and they crawled in, took their clothes off, and sat on the soft cedar branches.

"Smell good here." Ahni said as Mam poured a bit of water on the rocks. Steam filled the little area warming them to their very toes. "Smell like cedar tea. I like it here," Ahni said.

Mam took her hand and wrote. I-d-o-t-o-o.

Ahni spent the rest of the daylight hours with Mam, Ellie, Tarmo, and some of the loggers who had all come from Finland. Mam wrote in Ahni's hand. G-r-a-m-m-y-f-r-o-m-F-i-n-l-a-n-d. Ahni told the group what Mam had written.

"Hyvä. You're a Finnish girl. I should've been able to tell that by how hard you work without complaining." Ahni learned that the man talking was Matti and he'd been a sailor with a Swedish shipping company. He hadn't liked how he was treated aboard ship and the poor food he had to eat, so when the ship docked in New York, he left. Little by little he'd made his way west. Actually, he'd hoped to get to a place called California. "Maybe, someday, I'll still get there. I hear it's sunny and warm all year round."

"How're you going to get there? Walk? It's a long way away, I've heard," said Tarmo.

"I've heard plenty of stories about wagon trains heading to California. Whole families are going. Babies are even born along the way. I just have to get to the state of Missouri. People and their wagons join up in a town called Independence in the spring and head west together. I'm figuring on offering to help with the cattle or whatever so I don't have to buy a wagon and oxen. Without those, yup, I guess I'll be doing a lot of walking."

Tarmo asked, "How long does it take to get to California with all those wagons, women, children, cattle, and the like?"

"Word is that it's about five or six months depending on if there's good weather or bad. When a wheel breaks on a wagon, there's a delay to fix it. They stop to rest at night and get a good meal. And then there are the Indians. Some don't want white men coming and killing the buffalo for sport. Sometimes the hunters leave the whole carcass to rot. There are some Indians who help get the wagons across rivers and even scout the best routes that have drinkable water along the way."

"What do you think?" Tarmo asked Ellie. "Should we pull up stakes before we get too comfortable here and head out to California where it's always warm and sunny?"

"Not on your life! We come from people who live in the icy and snowy north. Why would we want sunny and warm every day?"

"Might be nice," Tarmo said, "but I'm not so sure about walking for five months or trying to get enough money together for a wagon, or a team of horses . . . unless Mr. Woods wouldn't mind if I borrowed a few from him and then forgot to return them once I got to sunny California."

Just then, with a whoop and a holler, Harry announced that the venison was roasted and it was time to chow. Three men helped him hoist it from over the pit fire and onto a table they'd dragged out from the mess. Harry sharpened a long knife on a whetstone then began to slice juicy chunks from the haunches of the deer. The men jostled for position to get their share. When Mam and Ahni got to the head of the line, Harry smiled at them and whispered, "Tenderloin chops." Then he sliced generous chunks from a piece that he pulled out by the ribs.

They ate with Ellie, Tarmo, and Matti, all who shared tender meat from the same loin. "Harry must like us." Matti said, "He only gives the tenderloin to special people."

"Not *us*," said Tarmo. "I suspect it's someone else he likes."

Ellie nudged him in the ribs, "Don't go starting something you don't know anything about."

"I know plenty. It doesn't have to be words. I can read eyes, smiles, and who gets the best tender cuts of venison and who doesn't."

Ahni looked around the group and said, "It's me he like. He say he give me something special later."

Mam looked uncomfortable. She kept her head down and ate her venison.

While the Finns were talking about wagon trains and dreaming about the promises of California, another group began singing songs from their homeland. "They're from Sweden," Matti said. "Some of those guys are not so bad, but one—that Espen guy—likes to do a lot of preaching. When he starts, I pretend I don't understand a word of what he says, and that's not stretching the truth too far. His English isn't all that good."

"Ya," said a stocky Finn named Asko, "I heard he came here looking to make a fortune sending furs back to his home country. That didn't happen so he's here chopping and sawing six days a week like the rest of us. And, as he says, 'bringing us the good word.' Hah! You should hear some of the *good words* he says when a tree he's felling doesn't land where he'd hoped. And that happens often."

The men laughed, but then became silent listening to the next song. Ahni felt sleepy sitting around the bonfire and listening to the singing and story-telling. She wished the sun would lower in the sky so the loggers would head back to their bunk houses. Then she could find out what Harry had promised for a surprise.

Before that happened, Matti said, "Hey, you know what I haven't done since the old country?"

"I can think of a lot of things, but you tell us what you're thinking," Tarmo said with a smile as Ellie poked him in the ribs.

"I was thinking . . ."

"Stop right there," Asko said laughing. "We already know that you haven't done any thinking since getting here."

"Let me finish! I was thinking that it would be fun to do the blanket toss. The beautiful Ahni has been here for almost a week, and we haven't done the blanket toss once!"

A chorus of the loggers' voices rang out. "Yo! *Hauskaa aikaa! Hupi*!!!" Time to have some fun. Ahni had no idea what a blanket toss was, and it didn't seem like something to get excited about. They'd just be tossing a blanket back and forth. What fun was that?

Ellie explained while someone ran to get a blanket. Most of the loggers joined in and held onto the edges of the blanket. Ellie told Ahni to stand in the middle. Soon she was flying in the air. Jovial voices rang out encouragement in various languages. *Hurra! Roligt! Högre! Plus haute! Korkeampi! Vielä kerras!*

Ahni felt a thrill going through her whole body each time the loggers threw her to the sky and then caught her in the blanket. "Wheee!" she called out, not wanting the feeling of flying like a bird to ever end. She flapped her arms pretending they were wings. She peddled her legs hoping to reach greater heights. She breathed the chill air and watched the sun sink below the tree tops.

A cloud covered the sky for a moment as Ahni was tossed high. She looked to the tree tops. There she saw a figure. A man with a mossy-looking beard. He looked like he was woven into the branches—an almost invisible man. He didn't smile. He just looked at Ahni. His eyes glinted as the cloud passed over, and the sun struck him. Ahni was going to point to him and call out for everyone to look, but he had already disappeared into the branches.

CHAPTER 9

Dizzy and elated from flying through the air, Ahni almost didn't want the blanket toss to end, but she had something else to look forward to. Harry had promised something special. The day was ending. Clothes had been washed and were hanging to dry draped over bunk posts and over chair backs near the wood-stove heaters. A few loggers still headed to the little steam baths to wash themselves for the week ahead. Ahni breathed the chill air, filling her lungs. Mam and Harry stood together smiling at her. Tarmo picked her up, "Upsie," he said and swung her in a circle.

Ellie said, "Enough now. Before we know it, Sunday will be over. The loggers will head to the woods, and we'll be making bread and pealing mountains of potatoes."

"Don't remind us. Sundays should be twice as long as any of the other days."

At the end of the day, Harry warned Ahni and the rest of the kitchen crew not to eat anything while the loggers were chowing down the sausages and sucking marrow out of the deer bones he'd put out for them. "Why not? I hungry," Ahni asked.

"Can't tell. Wouldn't be a surprise if I did." Harry said before he went to the store room and came back with a handful of onions.

"Onions for surprise?" Ahni made a face.

"Ya. Onions are part of the surprise."

Ahni was sure she wasn't going to be happy with Harry's surprise. *Onions!*

When the mess hall was empty except for the kitchen crew and Tarmo, Harry said, "Time for you all to wait at a table. Your supper will be ready soon." He began chopping onions. Impatient, Ahni wished she were still flying high with loggers ready to catch her on the blanket while laughing and cheering in all their different languages. But then she remembered the man in the branches and shivered.

Mam sat with Ellie and Tarmo. Alfred had taken a sausage and left saying he was going to join a card game in the bunkhouse. He wanted no part of chopping and frying onions. Ahni put her head on the table and, if her stomach had not growled with hunger, she would have fallen asleep.

Harry cut and chopped something he hid behind a stack of pots so they couldn't see what it was. Ahni heard a sizzle as he put that something he was hiding into a cast iron pan on the stove. Then glorious smells, even those of onions, made Ahni's mouth water. *Maybe this be good surprise after all!*

"I put plates out," she called to Harry.

"Not yet, you just want to look-see at what's cooking."

He was right.

Tarmo's nose twitched. "I can guess what he's making."

"I know for sure what he's making," Ellie laughed. She tapped her chest and then lower.

Tarmo laughed. "That's it. I wondered what he'd done with those."

"Tell me. Tell me." Ahni tapped her chest and then lower as Ellie had. Mam smiled. "What this mean?" She tapped again.

Just then Harry called out, "Ahni, now you can come and be the first to load up your plate."

She ran to the cook stove and held out her plate. It didn't look so good—brown chunks of something with onions, but it smelled wonderful, and her stomach gave a little growl. Her mouth watered anticipating something delicious. Harry gave her a heaping scoopful. "What smell good, but look not good?" she asked.

Harry laughed, "Just eat, I'll tell you later."

They all sat together at the boss' table. "Mmmm. Good." Ahni scooped some more into her mouth and didn't say another word until she was finished licking her plate. Everyone else cleaned their plates of every morsel, every fried slice of onion, too. The only sounds had been, "*Mmmmm, more.*"

After the last bit was eaten, Ahni asked, "What so good with onions?"

"Flora, Ahni, and I will do the dishes while Ellie and Tarmo go get the last surprise of the day," Harry smiled and handed Ahni a towel to wipe the table with.

"More surprise good, but what so good I ate?" Ahni asked as she cleaned the table where they'd eaten.

"Just wait. You'll find out."

The dishes were almost done when Tarmo and Ellie came in carrying two long gunny sacks stuffed with hay. They laid them by the cook stove. "Your mattresses. No more sleeping on the hard floor." Ellie said.

Mam hugged Ellie. Tarmo said, "Harry's idea. He got the sacks. I stuffed them with hay and Ellie stitched them up so the hay wouldn't sneak out."

"Whee!" Ahni plopped down on one. "Nice. Thank so much. You good to us. Feed us. Give us good bed. Just need to know one thing. What was so good eating?"

Tarmo answered, "Remember that deer we roasted today?"

"Yup, delicious. Almost as good as that onion and what else?"

Tarmo tapped his chest as Ellie had, "Heart." He tapped lower. "Liver. Harry saved the heart and liver from the deer, chopped and fried them up with the onions for us. Best part of the deer."

Ahni scrunched up her nose and said, "Good thing you no tell me. Heart an' liver. I need remember that. Never tasted anything so good. You goin' huntin' agin soon?" Ahni held her hand to her heart. "Never heard of eatin' heart before."

Harry grinned as he said, "That's because you've never eaten at a lop-sided wooden table in my very fancy cook shack before."

The rest of the evening, they sat around the huge cook stove keeping warm. Harry made Ahni a mug of cedar tea. He took a sip from a bottle before passing it to Tarmo who passed it to Ellie. Mam didn't drink from the bottle, so Harry made her tea, too.

While Ahni remembered the good things that happened that day, she also shuddered a bit thinking of the man she saw high in the tall spruce tree. *Had she really seen a man entangled in the branches?*

She took a long sip of her tea and in a quivery voice asked, "Anyone see man in tree while I high up during blanket tossed?"

"Was it one of the loggers?"

"No. Think not. Look old. Too old for woods workin'. Had beard like made of moss. Kinda green with stuff in it. Coat like tree bark. One leg wound 'round branch. Other one 'round tree trunk. Arms 'round other branches. Cloud make him look shadowy. Cloud leave, His eyes glow in sun. Lookin' right at me. Scary stare."

No one laughed at her description. No one said her eyes must have been playing tricks on her as she was tossed high into the air. Mam slid her arm around Ahni's shoulders and looked sad. Everyone looked sad. Their happiness drained away. They all looked like a cloud had settled over them, too.

Finally, Tarmo said, "Could be she saw the *Wiindigoo* the Ojibwe talk about. Could be the *Nalka* we Finns watch out for in the forest. Could be something else. No one else saw it?"

Everyone shook their head. No.

"Scared me. Pap tole me because I born when moon covered sun an' alla land was dark alla roun', that I born to somethin' bad. But Grammy, she hold me tight in her arms an' call me *Dear Sweet Lamb-i-kins* an' say born during eclipse meant I born to something good. Mebbe that man coming' here is the somethin' good like Grammy said or somethin' bad like Pap said."

CHAPTER 10

That night when Mam and Ahni settled on their hay-filled beds, Ahni said to Mam, "I know the *Wiindigoo* always hungry an' eat up people, an' *Nalka* do scary things, too."

It was dark by the cook stove where they slept, but Mam took Ahni's hand in hers and drew the letters for what she wanted to say.

B-e c-a-r-e-f-u-l. N-o g-o o-u-t-s-i-d-e a-l-o-n-e.

"Why I not go outside alone? Have to use slop bucket in stables times you busy."

N-a-l-k-a t-a-k-e c-h-i-l-d-r-e-n N-e-v-e-r s-e-e a-g-a-i-n.

Ahni didn't understand, so Mam had to draw the letters again, slower so Ahni could say each word when she finished it. Nalka. Take. Children. Never. See. Again.

"Why he want children?"

Mam just wrote. *D-o-n-t k-n-o-w.*

"Maybe Tarmo and Ellie know. I ask them more 'bout *Nalka*. Kalle an' 'nother man tole me little bits that *Nalka* be woods giant. No worry, Mam, I no get lost in woods. Grammy said *Nalka* bad, too."

Ahni had told her mother not to worry, but Ahni worried. The man in the trees had stared hard at her. Remembering, her chin trembled. When she closed her eyes to sleep, the image of him wrapped around the trunk and woven in amongst the branches made her heart race. Afraid the scary man would come to her in dreams, she reached out to hold onto her mother.

Every noise that night, every branch that scraped the roof of the cook shack, every little snort her mother gave out at the end of a deep breath, woke up Ahni from her fitful sleep.

When Harry came in before dawn and started rattling pans, Mam got right up and gently shook Ahni's shoulder. Sunday was over. Another week of hard work was about to begin.

Harry poured dried beans into a big kettle. "Alfred, bring in water from the pump. Alfred? Where's Alfred? That lazy bum had better not be hungover from booze or hooch, whatever they call it in the bunkhouse."

Ellie grabbed a bucket and said she'd get water and ask Tarmo to rouse Alfred out of his bunk. "Good," answered Harry. "Flora, start mixing batter for the flap-jacks. I've gotta get these sausages on the griddle. Ahni, you're going to have to watch them and turn them 'til Alfred gets here."

After returning with the water and helping Harry pour it into the bean pot to get them softening for the evening meal, Ellie started measuring flour and the other ingredients for the many loaves of bread they'd need that day.

Harry had just started the gallons of coffee that warmed up the loggers for their day in the woods when Tarmo came in. "Alfred's still not here?" Tarmo asked looking around the cook shack.

"Haven't seen hide nor hair of him," Harry answered.

"Neither have the guys in the bunkhouse. He didn't play cards with them last night. Or drink firewater with them. They hadn't seen him at all in the bunkhouse last night. His bunk wasn't even slept in."

"We all saw him yesterday when he grabbed a couple of sausages and left to play cards."

"That's the last I saw him."

"Maybe he's up to no good and played a trick on Ahni who saw him up in the tree."

"No. Not see Alfred in tree. Man up tree have eyes starin'. Scary. An' Alfred no have beard lookin' like moss. Man in tree do."

"I'll look for Alfred as soon as I finish watering and feeding the horses. Gotta get them all hitched up for the day." Tarmo shook his head, gave Ellie a little hug and left.

"Well, Ahni, and everyone else, Alfred might just be taking his time in the out-house, or he might be shirking his work. He hasn't been happy about washing dishes and scrubbing floors. We'll have more to do this morning if he doesn't show up soon. If everyone helps everyone else, we'll get it done."

After turning sausages on the griddle, Ahni scampered to carry plates, forks, and coffee mugs to the tables. She hurried back to the griddle to make sure the sausages were cooking evenly. Back and forth she ran. *Good thing I got used to this last week.*

After the loggers came in to eat, Ahni ran from table to table bringing platters of flapjacks. Ellie helped by carrying the heavy coffee pots to the tables and filling mugs. Mam brought out sausages while Harry carried bowls of a sauce made of dried raisins and prunes. While the men ate, Ahni helped Ellie and Mam make sandwiches for the men to carry with them for their noon meal to the woods. Harry piled apples into a big pail for the men to take, too.

Ahni thought about her first day at the camp and how every muscle in her arms and legs had ached and how she had been ready drop to the wooden floor weeping with weariness. She was now actually enjoying the fast pace and even skipped a bit while carrying an empty plate to the dish washing tub. Even though Alfred still hadn't come, she didn't mind thinking about washing dishes and all the other clean-up she would have to do. That was because she would get to eat all she wanted for breakfast and would be working with Harry, Ellie, and Mam. She looked forward to Tarmo coming back in after he was done in the stables.

After the men left for the woods, Harry shook his head and said, "Dang that Alfred. Leaving us in the lurch like this. He'd better come in crawling on his hand and knees and with his last breath tell me that he has dysentery, pneumonia, or some other deadly disease. And then I'll gladly hitch him to one of the horses and have him pulled into the woods for Old Biddy Bones to heal."

Ahni had cleared the tables and was wiping them clean. "Who Old Biddy Bones?"

"Old Biddy Bones is a scrawny old woman who, if you believe the tall tales the lumberjacks tell, can stir up a concoction of roots, leaves, grasses, bees wax, mud from a river bottom and whatever else she needs to cure whatever ails you."

"I don't believe there is such a real person!" Ellie was already scooping a heap of flour into a huge wooden dough box. "Ahni, would you run to the store room and get me the salt? Dizzy me forgot to grab it while I was getting the flour."

"She maybe was real at one time," Harry said. "Maybe she still is. Most tall tales are about real people with a few exaggerations here and there."

"Tell more 'bout Old Biddy Bones." Ahni handed Ellie the salt, then went to get a broom from the little closet so she could start sweeping.

"Some say Old Biddy Bones is so terrifying to look at that when a sick person goes to be healed, one look at her chases the sickness right out of 'em. They run out the door cured of their fever. Broken bones are even healed instantly. Looking at her even scares pustules off their bodies! All healed!"

Ellie laughed, and Mam broke out in a big smile. "What makes her so creepy to look at?"

Ahni was wondering the same so was glad Ellie had asked.

"To start with, she's earned her name well—Old Biddy Bones. She is so scrawny that she's just skin stretched over bones. The color of her skin looks like flames—as red as blood. If that isn't terrifying enough, she has one green eye and one yellow. Her long, crooked nose ends in something like a raven's claw. Some say she has six fingers on each hand!"

Tarmo came in just then. "Harry, did anyone ever tell you that the stories you make up are as good as your cooking?"

"I'll pretend that's a compliment," Harry said. "Now, let's eat breakfast so we can get busy."

"Still no Alfred?" asked Tarmo. "I've checked the whole camp area. I have no clue where he might be."

"When it gets light out, we can check to see if any tracks lead out of the camp." Harry handed Mam a ladle so she could scoop flapjack batter on the griddle. Ellie checked to see if there was enough coffee.

"I can't wait for Sunday and blanket toss again," Ahni tugged on Tarmo's arm.

He picked Ahni up and twirled her twice. "We have long days of lots of work before then, but it's something to look forward to," Tarmo said as he put her down.

In the weak wintery dawn, the kitchen crew scoured the grounds around all the buildings. Fresh snow had covered any tracks that might lead into the woods except for the trail made by the horses, sledges, and men that headed north to their logging site.

Tarmo and Harry followed that trail to see if there were any prints veering off from the well-used path. Ellie, Mam, and Ahni stayed behind. They searched the bunkhouse. Each bunk was just piles of hay on top of boards and covered with a red and black blanket. Ahni punched the hay to make sure Alfred wasn't hiding there and then crawled under each lower bunk. She didn't find anything but dirty socks and dust. Next, they knocked on the door of the outhouse. No one answered, so they creaked the door open. Empty.

The stables were bigger and harder to search, but Ahni delighted in the warmth and smell the horses had left behind. She jumped on piles of hay to make sure Alfred wasn't hidden under them. She pretended he was as she leapt into stack after stack. "Alfred, you lazy bones. I jump on yer head! I bust yer bones ifn you be sleepin' instead of scrubbin.'"

Elli helped Ahni by poking a pitch fork into piles of hay. "He'll come running our fast enough after one jab of this," she laughed. Meanwhile, Mam checked the corner that held gunny sacks of feed. They all looked to the rafters, but no Alfred balanced on the wooden poles.

Ahni even crawled into each of the cedar branch-covered sweat lodges to see if he was curled asleep in them. No Alfred. Just before going back to the cook shack, Ahni looked to the tall spruce trees where she'd seen the man with the glowing eyes staring at her. She half hoped to see Alfred sprawled on the branches hiding from them. She also hoped she would not see the mossy bearded man with his arms and legs woven into the branches. To her relief, she saw the spruce branches sway gentle in the wind. A scruffy raven landed where the man had been the day before. Snow shook from a branch as it fluttered its wings to settle down. The raven looked at Ahni, or at least she thought so. A cloud covered the sun, and the wind picked up ruffling the raven's feathers. With a hoarse *gronk*, it flew away.

"Well," Ellie said, "I guess we might as well go inside to warm up. We haven't seen a single thing that would tell us where Alfred went. We still have all the dishes to wash, bread to make, and supper to get going."

Every evening meal in the logging camp was either bean soup, pea soup, or stew. Ellie, Mam, and Ahni peeled and chopped potatoes, rutabagas, and carrots before putting them into the big pots that simmered with the peas or beans. The bread was heavy, crusty and dark from a big scoop of molasses Ellie poured into the dough. Chunks of ham as well as ham hocks were always in the soups. If was a stew night, Harry stirred the chopped root vegetables in with chunks of fat sausages. Then he brought a couple cabbages out of the store room and chopped them into the stew, too.

Beans were already in water softening for that night's soup. Ellie and Harry argued about what sweet to make for the day. Harry said, "Pie. The men like pie. Apple pie with raisins or cranberries. And we have lots of pumpkins piled in the store room along with some monstrous squash. They make good pie, too.

Ellie crossed her arms across her chest and said, "The men might like bread pudding for a change. Leftover bread crusts, wrinkled apples, a handful of cranberries or raisins, topped with molasses. The men'll gobble it up."

"I like both," Ahni's mouth watered just thinking about the sweet desserts.

"What do you like?" Harry asked Mam hoping he'd side with him.

"Mam took Ahni's hand and wrote, F-r-u-i-t s-a-u-c-e. A-p-p-l-e c-r-a-n-b-e-r-r-i-e-s.

Ahni said, "Mam an' Grammy made fruit sauce with apples an' berries an' handful of brown sugar or molasses to sweeten. It so good." She licked her lips and remembered the good days. The days before Big Thunder died. Before Pap became a drunk. Before they were hungry all the time.

"Well, fruit sauce it is. Ahni, take a basket and fill it with withered apples. It'll be up to you to cut them into quarters and dig out the cores. They don't need to be peeled if they're going to get all mashed up in the sauce."

Mam and Ellie got busy kneading the day's bread dough while Harry brought out the ham hocks, potatoes and carrots for the bean soup. He dropped the hocks in a bucket of water to draw out some of the saltiness before putting them into the soup kettle.

"Looks like the fruit sauce is a good idea," Ellie said. "We don't have to make crusts or chop up dried bread for pudding. We might even get some rest time today." She and Flora set the big wooden dough box near the warm stove so the dough would rise faster.

The following morning, chores went smoothly. Even without Alfred, the cook shack crew got their work done and had time to relax. Tarmo and Axel had gone to the river to see if they could find any tracks that Alfred might have made if he'd gone that way. They returned with a couple of nice fish they'd speared through a hole they'd chopped in the ice.

"Look what we brought for lunch. Too bad we don't have a net. Might be able to trap more fish that way. With the river freezing over we'd have to use it right away, but we could entangle enough for a good fish stew for a supper." Axel stomped snow off his boots as he talked.

Harry got busy scaling the two good-sized fish. "Pan fried fish coming up! If Alfred is anywhere near, he'll hear it sizzling in the pan and smell it frying and come running."

The mention of Alfred darkened everyone's mood. Where could he have gone, leaving no trace?

CHAPTER 12

Snow fell softly as the loggers came in for the evening meal. They shook the flakes off their shoulders and hats while stomping their boots.

"Another week in the wilds chopping down trees and freezing our hands and feet. For what? More bean soup!"

"You tell 'em, Espen!" Sven, tapped his friend on the shoulder with his mitts as they sat at the table with other loggers who'd come from the same country and spoke the same language.

The kitchen crew rushed to get food on the tables.

"Anyone see anything of Alfred?" Sven slurped his soup.

"Not a thing. We looked for footprints, a trail that went off into the woods, any-thing, but found no sign of him," said Harry.

Axel shook his head. "I looked all over the place for him, too. This isn't good. We can't have men going off and getting lost like this. Mr. Woods isn't going to like it at all. Next thing you know, everyone'll be telling wild stories about what happened to him." He pointed to the men and said in a booming voice, "No starting spook stories. We don't want this camp getting a bad reputation." He looked at Ahni and scowled.

When Axel sat down, the loggers began scooping soup into their mouths. Every once in a while, one would nudge the man next to him, and they'd watch Ahni as she carried platters of bread to the tables. They'd look down quickly if she looked at them. Quietly muttering, some whispered things like, ". . . eclipse. Bad born. Saw strange man in trees. Maybe a monster. Now Alfred's gone. Watch out. Don't get on her bad side. You might be next."

Ahni felt eyes following her as she brought more soup to each table. She heard the whispers. *Were they blaming her for Alfred's disappearance?* She felt a flutter in her chest and her face flushed red. Even Axel looked at her as though accusing her. She hadn't done anything wrong . . . except be born when the moon covered the sun during the day. She couldn't help that. She wished her Grammy was there to hold her close and call her *Dear Sweet Lamb-i-kins.*

That night, after the loggers left, Ahni sat at the bosses' table with the rest of the cook crew and Tarmo. They talked about how they'd handle all the chores now that Alfred was gone.

Ahni couldn't hold her tongue any longer. "I no do nothin' to make Alfred gone!"

Ellie looked surprised. "We know that. Why do you say that?"

"Loggers be talkin' an' lookin' at me. Saying' I be born with *'clipse* and be trouble."

"That's just logger talk," Tarmo put a hand over Ahni's. "They're way out in the woods all winter without their families. They suffer from the cold every day. Their work is dangerous. They tell stories to entertain themselves. After they've told and heard all the old stories, they start making new ones up. Some believe eclipses are bad omens. Some even believe that having a woman in the camp is bad luck, and they've never been in a camp with a young girl before. Alfred's gone missing, so they're making up a story about you."

"Ya," said Harry. "Loggers have a reputation of being superstitious, so any little thing sets them off."

"I'll talk to Reino and see if he can talk to the loggers and get this mumbling stopped." Tarmo took his hand from Ahni's and scratched his chin. "Let's hope no one else runs away or goes missing. Then we'd have real trouble."

Ahni still felt sad the next morning as she ran back and forth getting raisins and molasses for the oatmeal and carrying bowls and spoons to the tables. She tried to forget the whisperings of the men the night before, but they'd kept her awake half the night. She wished she'd never told anyone about being born while an eclipse darkened the skies or seeing the man in the tree.

Something else wasn't right that morning either. Mam dragged her feet as she set about doing her morning chores. She rested often while beating scoops of flour, water, and molasses for the day's bread. Ellie even noticed. "Aren't you feeling well?" she asked.

Harry looked over when Ellie asked that. Mam did look pale and tired. "Didn't you sleep well?"

Mam signaled that nothing was wrong. She tried to speed up her work, but she was tired. Something bothered her. When she thought about it, she hadn't had her moon flow for two months. She tried to shrug it off as not having enough to eat when she'd been home, and working harder than ever while at the logging camp. She felt her stomach. No bump, but when she'd carried Ahni, she hadn't shown for about four months. She counted on her fingers. If she was two months pregnant, it would be April or May when the new baby was born. She hoped with all her might that no baby was growing in her belly.

Creases formed in her forehead as she wondered if Harry would send her away if he found out she was pregnant. She didn't want to leave. Not in the middle of the winter. Not to go back to the man who'd turned so cruel after he could no longer go to the woods to cut wood. She would not go back to scrabbling for scraps of food. And, if she admitted it to herself, she'd miss Harry who was as kind as her husband was cruel. She'd also miss Ellie and Tarmo. She wished for a relationship like theirs. With Harry that might be possible.

After breakfast was over and everything cleaned for the evening meal, Mam took a break to look at the calendar Ellie had hung on the wall and crossed each day off as soon as they were done for the night and ready to blow out the candles.

"What you looking at?" Ahni asked.

C-a-l-e-n-d-a-r. Mam wrote on Ahni's hand.

Ellie came over, "Are you counting the days until the spring thaw when the camp will be closed, and we all can go home?"

"Lemme read calendar. Never see one afore."

Ellie pointed to the day's date. "It's the fifth day of November." She pointed to the big letters at the top of the page and to the number 5. And look here, we have Wednesday, Thursday, Friday, and Saturday to cross off before we get to Sunday again."

Ahni repeated all the days of the week as Ellie pointed to them again. Back home they'd never paid attention to days and months. They'd just lived according to what the weather was like. Ahni knew it was spring when little frogs peeped in the swamp. Violets and dandelions bloomed in their small yard. Different birds came to build nests in trees. Spring was followed by the warm days of summer and berry picking. That was when the lakes and rivers were warm enough for swimming. Best of all was what Grammy called autumn because they got to pick wild apples and everything in their tiny garden.

"How long winter last?" Ahni turned the pages to December and January.

Ellie turned two more pages. "February and March are winter months, too. Hopefully the thaw will start then and the ground will be too soft for the horses to pull the sledges full of heavy logs. That's when we go home!"

"Everyone go home? What happen to camp when nobody here?"

Harry came to stand by them. "I'll come back to camp after the log drive. I don't have family or home to go back to, so I'll stay to help take the big oven apart. The big mess hall stove, too. The parts will get loaded on a wagon and brought to the new camp site. We'll take some other things, too. The doors, windows, all the tools—anything we can't make at the new site."

"Why go new place? Here is good."

"By the end of winter, we'll have taken down all the trees that we want for a big area around here, so we move closer to a forest that hasn't been cut and spend the summer building stables, bunkhouse, and cook shack. About eight of us stay and do all that. Besides, I do the cooking for them, too."

"Don't need Ellie, Tarmo, Mam, and me?"

"We'd like you all to stay, but no, with a smaller crew and no logging to be done other than cutting trees for the new buildings, we don't need more people. Mr. Woods wouldn't pay extra folks or provide for their food, either."

None of that sounded good to Ahni. Where would she and Mam go? She missed Grammy, but not Pap.

CHAPTER 13

Ahni watched Ellie tear the November page from her calendar. She was happy to see that in two more days, December third, was a Sunday. She was also glad she hadn't seen the man in the tree again, and that the men had quit looking at her and whispering about her having something to do with Alfred going missing. Axel, the camp boss, had left two days ago to get more supplies and to meet with Mr. Woods. She hoped he'd be back in time for Sunday and that he'd bring lots of good things.

Harry had given Axel a list of supplies he needed to keep the loggers fed. Harry had wiped sweat off his forehead as he told Axel, "Be sure to tell boss man that we need more help. We're running everyone ragged here in the kitchen."

Tarmo had also given a list for horse feed. And Reino said "A saw has gone missing since Alfred left. An axe, too. It'd be nice to have a new saw or two on hand in case an old one snaps."

One thing worried Ahni. Mam was tired all the time. Ellie tried to get her to sit and rest, but Mam refused, so Ellie had whispered to Ahni that she needed to help Mam whenever she could. Ahni herself was tired all the time and was glad it soon would be Sunday. Bath time and there was already another deer hanging behind the bunkhouse waiting to be roasted.

Sunday morning was cloudy and blustery, but that couldn't dampen Ahni's wishes for a fun day and another blanket toss. "I hope Axel gets back today or tomorrow."

Harry frowned as he dropped an armload of breakfast food on the plank table. "We'll be running out of ham and sausages before the month is over. Slim pickings are what we're left with. Ellie, know any good squash or pumpkin recipes so we can start using more of those?"

"They can be chopped up for soups and stews. Or mashed with lard to make flat cakes to fry. Other than that, they're good for pies and puddings."

Wind rattled the one window in the cook shack. Branches scratched the roof. "Sounds like the *Wiindigoo* wants to get in," Harry joked.

"Not funny." Ellie swatted him with a towel. "Don't you dare say that in front of some of the loggers or you'll get them telling those scary stories again."

After breakfast, the weather worsened. A few loggers went outside to light fires in the steam baths and build the outdoor fires for warming tubs of wash water. Most stayed in the mess playing cards or telling stories.

"Ever hear the one about that bigger than life logger named Paul Bunyan?" asked Swen.

"About a hunnerd times. Don't want to hear no logging stories on Sunday," Asko called from the other table.

"Well, as long as there are so many of us here, I'll take this opportunity to read stories from the Good Book instead of waiting 'til later when everyone pretends they have something else to do." Espen pulled a black book out of his jacket. "I'll read about a man—a giant warrior, who had armor and spear, but he was taken down by a young boy named David who only had a stone. Good story. Something we should remember."

As soon as he started to read, most of the loggers found other things to do. The few who stayed to listen agreed that it was a good story. "The weak can take down the strong," one murmured when the story was over. "You just have to out-smart 'em."

The wind blew harder, and the snow deepened. The deer roasted over the outdoor fire, baths were taken, and clothes washed, but the men didn't laugh or joke with each other. Worse yet, the wind was so gusty that they didn't toss Ahni up and down on the blanket. Harry did save loin meat, heart, and liver for the cook crew, but that was about the only good thing happening that day.

In the afternoon, Ahni sat with the Ojibwe and Finn loggers at their table. Harry brought a big kettle of hot water and Tarmo laid an arm load of cedar branches on the table. Everyone poured themselves a mug of hot water then tore off a few cedar sprigs to steep into an aromatic tea. Ahni listened to the stories the Finns told as she sipped her tea.

Most had been born in the "old country," but left because they had no farm lands of their own to work. They'd heard about America where there was plenty of land to be had.

As the men described the huge ships they came on, Ahni imagined Grammy sailing on one of those big ships, too.

Kalle said, "Must have been at least 200 people on my ship. Half of them, like me, were crammed into the lowest deck or steerage. Many of us had to squeeze into a small space. We could hardly move. The bunks were three high. Two slept in each one. I had to share a bunk with a sickly man who moaned and groaned every time the ship rocked with the waves which was most of the time. The man died before we were even two weeks out of port." He shook his head thinking of how awful his journey had been.

"That's no lie. Steerage was horrible." Matti rubbed his hands over his head remembering the suffering on the ship he'd crossed the Atlantic on. "We were treated worse than cattle. They told us the trip would only take six weeks or so, but we had such bad weather for days on end that it took us twice as long. Those of us in steerage had been told to bring our own food. As the trip grew longer, people ran out of food. Fights broke out every day. I had to keep a hold on my food sack every minute if I didn't want it stolen. The steerage was so damp, everyone's bread turned moldy within a few days. I was lucky to have brought hard tack and chunks of cheese. When I thought most everyone was asleep and couldn't hear me, I tore the mold off the cheese and softened the hard tack in my mouth instead of biting into it and making noise. I didn't want anyone knowing I still had food left, but it was probably harder to keep the rats out of my cheese than it was to fight off the other people."

Asko fingered the rip in the sleeve of his plaid shirt. "I was on one of those steam ships, too. The weather held most of my trip so it only took about seven weeks, but by the end of my trip, I was not only starving but had lice and dysentery. I could barely walk by the time the ship landed in Nova Scotia."

Everyone was quiet for a while after the men finished their stories of the hardships crossing the Atlantic to get to the Americas. Both Matti and Asko told of over forty people in steerage dying during their crossing. The weather had been so bad on Kalle's trip that the hatches had been locked from above so there was no way to get out of steerage to even get a breath of fresh air.

"We couldn't even carry the dead to the deck for burial at sea. We had to pile the bodies in one corner until we could carry them to an upper deck. With the hatches locked, we couldn't get to the only bathroom on the next deck up so we used buckets that tipped over and spilled every time the ship rocked with a big wave. That putrid mess spread over the whole floor. Everyone had to stay in their bunks and suffer the stench, the dark, and dampness. No wonder so many died. I thought for sure that I would, too." Kalle shuddered.

Ahni listened intently. She tried to imagine boats so big that they held 200 or more people. She couldn't even imagine a big water like the men called the Atlantic Ocean that would take weeks and months to cross. She knew what an outhouse smelled like. She couldn't imagine living with that every day, but she could imagine the hunger they'd suffered.

That night as Ellie crossed off the third day of December before heading to the stables with Tarmo for the night, Ahni said, "Maybe December not so good."

"We could be in for lots more snow and storms," Harry said. "Winter is still four more months. We're so far north, we're almost in that land called Canada. This far north is known for wicked winters. Let's get some sleep tonight and hope that Axel doesn't get snowed in anywhere making him late getting back."

Ahni settled down on her straw-filled sack for the night thinking about the stories the men had told and wishing it had been a sunny day so she could have soared in the air during a blanket toss.

CHAPTER 14

Axel did not get back to the camp the next day. Meanwhile, the snow piled up and the wind whistled through tree tops.

"Not going to be a good day in the woods," complained the men as they downed huge stacks of hot flapjacks and bowls of apple-raisin sauce. "Dangerous as can be with the wind blowing this hard."

Big John and White Wolf shook their heads when Reino the woods boss stood from his table and headed for the door. It was time for the men to follow and start trudging through the new snow to the logging site. Ahni liked Big John and White Wolf. They were wiry Ojibwes who never missed a chance to smile and thank her. She, in return, always brought them platters stacked the highest with flapjacks, and the bowls of sauce thick with chopped fruit. At first, they'd been a mystery to her. They both wore their hair long and braided. They wore deerskin coats over their woolen shirts. Their hats were different, too. The other men wore knitted woolen hats, but Big John wore a hat made of a fox tail, and White Wolf's was white fur.

That night when the men returned tired and snow-covered from the woods, Ahni asked White Wolf as he shook snow from his hat, "That wolf fur?"

"Ya," he said. "Do you want to learn how to say *wolf* in my language?"

"Ya," she said, using the word most loggers used.

"Ma'iingan." White Wolf smiled.

"Ma'iigan. Ma'iingan," Ahni repeated. The word was strange on her tongue, but she like softness of the word. Saying it was like a song.

"Tomorrow, I'll teach you to say *White Wolf.*"

"Teach me now. I practice all night. In morning I say it good."

All the men at the table laughed as they started scooping their bowls full of the hot venison stew. "*Waabishki-ma'iingan.* My name given by elders when *nimaamaa* died giving birth to me."

Big John added, "A white wolf howled and paced around our village on the day he was born. We believe the white wolf was saying it would take care of him now that he had no mother. We believe *Waabishki-ma'iingan* is White Wolf's spirit brother."

"That beautiful story," said Ahni. "I wish I had spirit brother. Story of my birth not so beautiful even though my mam lives."

"Tell us your story," Big John encouraged.

"Bad story. People think I born bad. Cause trouble. Maybe make Alfred run away or go missing. Maybe monster like *Wiindigooo* or *Nalka* get him 'cuz I be born bad."

"Oh, ya. I heard some of the loggers saying you were born during an eclipse. It's just a superstition that if you're born when the moon covers the sun, you'll bring troubles. Don't worry about it and don't believe it yourself." Big John patted Ahni on the shoulder as he spoke.

Ahni felt better after Big John patted her. She ran faster than ever filling stew pots, loading more bread onto platters for the two tables, and finally bringing out the pudding Mam and Ellie had made with cranberries and apples.

Axel still hadn't returned with the supplies that night when Harry said, "Chores done. Let's get some sleep."

Ellie began blowing out candles while Tarmo brought in a huge armload of wood and set it by the cook stove. "It's nasty out there," he said. His nose and cheeks were as red as could be from the sharp wind. He nodded to Mam and Ahni saying, "You better wrap up good for your run outside to the stables. Ellie, leave one candle here in the kitchen so they can see when they get back."

Mam and Ahni followed Tarmo and Ellie to the stables. No stars shone. No moon lit their way. "Hold onto the rope!" Tarmo yelled over the whipping wind. Now Ahni understood why Tarmo had tied the ropes from one building to another earlier in the winter. She couldn't see a foot in front of herself, at moments she couldn't even see Mam who was right in back of her. She could easily have gotten lost and wandered around the camp never being able to see where she was going. *White-out* is what she'd heard Tarmo say to Harry earlier when he'd asked what it was like outside.

In the short time it took Ahni and her mother to buck the wind back to the cook shack, they'd just about frozen through and through. They huddled next to the big oven trying to thaw when Harry came out of the back storeroom where he had his cot. "There's lots of cedar sprays left. Let's heat water and have a last cup of tea before blowing out the candle for the night."

Besides the tea, Harry brought out some hard tack. Ahni dunked hers into her mug to soften it up a bit. Two front teeth had been bothering her. They were loose. Harry noticed her fingering them. "Getting ready to lose more teeth?" he asked.

"Think so," she replied. Mam signaled for Ahni to open her mouth and fingered the two teeth. She nodded and smiled at Ahni.

"How old are you, again?" asked Harry.

"Eight. I think." She looked at her mother.

Mam nodded.

"You work harder than any eight-year-old I've ever known. Have you lost any teeth yet?"

Ahni pulled down her lower lip so he could see where two teeth were slowly growing in where two other teeth had fallen out.

"Tell you what. When those two upper teeth fall out, we'll make a cake to celebrate. Hopefully, the storm will let up and Axel will be able to make it back tomorrow or the next day. He'll have more brown sugar for a cake. And Ellie knows how to whip up a good one. Your mam probably does, too. We'll leave it up to them."

Ahni smiled. Harry always made her feel so good. Mam was smiling at him, too. He said, "Ahni, time for you to sleep now. I want to stay up a bit longer with your mother so we can plan that tooth-celebrating cake."

Before falling asleep, Ahni said over and over *Waabishki-ma'iingan*. She wanted to sound like a song when she said it to White Wolf in the morning.

CHAPTER 15

During the night, the snow stopped, but the wind still howled eerily. Tree branches slapped the roof of the cook shack. The men shivered from the cold and kicked snow from their boots when they came in for breakfast. Ahni couldn't wait for White Wolf to sit at his table so she could say his name. *Waabishki-ma'inigan* she whispered to herself.

The loggers were still heading to their benches when Ahni almost tripped while carrying a steaming bowl of oatmeal to one of the tables. She caught herself from falling nose first, but the bowl flew from her hands, and the oatmeal spilled to the floor. "Watch where you're going!" Sven roared. Ahni looked at his big boot. She'd felt it hit her foot. It was still between her feet. "Better get that mopped up and bring another bowl to our table." Then Sven sat down, jabbed the fellow next to him and laughed.

Ahni was scooping up the spilled oatmeal when White Wolf and Big John came in. "We'll finish that while you get food on the tables." A man named Cloudy helped so in no time the oatmeal had been scraped up, and the floor mopped.

Later, Big John asked her what happened. "Think that Sven man purposely tripped me, but don't know for sure. Wasted food. Sven man holler at me. Now I feel bad."

Just then Reino the logging boss came in. "Finish eating. Daylight's coming, and we need to get on the job."

After the loggers left, Mam and Ellie got busy making bread, but Harry sat Ahni down and asked her what had happened. She told him she thought Sven had tripped her. Harry shook his head and said, "He's a sly one. Always making up stories about others. Tarmo says he causes trouble in the bunkhouse, too. Always rude and nasty to the Finns and Indians. Thinks he's better than them. There's even been some rumblings that he had something to do with Alfred leaving. Let me know if he does anything else to you."

Ahni felt better as she cleared the tables and washed dishes. When she was done, Harry told her to get an armload of pumpkins and start chopping them for pies.

When the loggers came in that evening, Sven sniffed the air. "Let me guess. It's either pea soup or bean soup. Anyone want to take a bet?"

No one did. Ahni made sure she stayed far from him as she carried kettles of pea soup to the tables. As usual, the loggers ate without talking until Mam helped Ahni carry out pies for dessert.

"Pumpkin pie! My favorite! Haven't had one for a while!"

"Dig in, men!" Harry called out. "We have plenty. Made by the delicate hands of Ahni, Flora, and Ellie! Treat them well, and maybe they'll have more surprises coming out of this oven for you!"

White Wolf and Cloudy smiled and patted their tummies as Ahni brought a third and fourth pie to their table. "We need to give her good Ojibwe name."

"I can say White Wolf's name," Ahni smiled proudly as she said, "*Waabishki-ma'iingan.* What's Cloudy in your language?"

"Oooh. My family called me *Aanakwad,* but my name is really White Cloud. That's a long word. White Cloud is *Waabishkaanakwad.*"

"*Waabishki* like in White Wolf's name?"

"Ya, it means *white.*"

Ahni tried saying it, but it came out all funny. "I keep trying," she said. "Soon I can say."

White Wolf took another piece of pie and said, "*Giiwedin-anong.* That's the name I'm giving you." Big John nodded, so did Cloudy.

"What mean?"

"North Star. You, like North Star. Very important."

After the loggers went to the bunkhouse for the night, Ahni helped measure flour for the next day's flapjacks. All the while she thought of the name *Giiwedinanong* and that White Wolf had said it was an important star. She forgot all about having been tripped by Sven and felt all warm inside that she had an important name and had helped make the pumpkin pies. She didn't even mind that Mam stayed up with Harry after she'd gone to bed.

Axel didn't arrive back at the camp on Wednesday, either. Everyone worried and fretted about what could have happened to him. Tarmo's forehead wrinkled as he said, "Bad weather and deep snow. He could be bogged down somewhere. His horse and sledge maybe couldn't get through some places, and the river isn't frozen enough to travel along."

Harry rubbed his chin as he always did when he was worried. "I hope he didn't try to travel the river. Back a few years when I still lived in the old country, my neighbor Juho Malinen was returning home with a horse-drawn wagon full of supplies. Because the snow was deep, he decided to travel the river. It was January already so he was sure it was safe. Well, he hit a weak spot in the ice. Down they went. The horse drowned, and all his supplies were lost. Luckily, Juho jumped off the wagon just in time, so he lived to tell about it."

The cook shack crew was settling down to eat a lunch of leftover oatmeal that Harry had sliced and fried when they heard a horse snort, a sledge creak, and a raspy voice call "Whoa!"

Everyone jumped up. Tarmo ran out to greet Axel. Ahni watched as Axel almost fell off the seat and fell into Tarmo's arms. By that time Harry was there and helped Axel into the cook shack. Tarmo unhitched the horse from the supply wagon and led it into the stables.

Mam and Ellie hustled around bringing Axel coffee and apple sauce. Harry fried some more oatmeal. Axel unwound the blanket he wore around his shoulders. "I'm about froze to death," were his first words. Ahni watched as he stepped closer to the big stove in the middle of the mess hall. His face reminded her of the story Harry told about Old Biddy Bones and her face being as red as flames. Axel's was red in places; white in others. "I got frost bitten for sure," he said. "My face felt really cold at first, but now it feels warm. That's not a good sign."

After he warmed up and had eaten, Axel told what had taken him so many days. "First of all, Mr. Woods wasn't in Port Charles at all. I met with one of his partners. He told me that vouchers had been left at the trading post, the feed depot, and the dry goods store and that I would have to figure out what I could buy with those and no more."

Harry shook his head. "Let me guess, it wasn't enough for everything we need."

"Not only that," Axel wiped his nose, "but he also didn't give me any money for the men. His exact words were 'No more paydays. Everyone will be paid all at once when we close up camp after the thaw starts.'"

"But . . ."

"That's exactly what I said. But . . ."

"The men aren't going to like this. I don't either. What if someone gets hurt and has to leave early? No pay for him? Only one big payday! And what if Mr. Big Boss doesn't come through with the money then?"

"I asked all that, but the partner said he was just telling what Mr. Woods had told him to say."

Ellie jumped into the conversation, "Well, we just have to hope and trust that we'll get paid. The big question now is, what were you able to get with the credit he allotted?"

"Not enough. The thing is, Mr. Woods's partner said he wasn't putting his money into logging anymore. He heard that a section of railroad has been built in Illinois—from Chicago to the galena mining area. Soon enough there'll be railroads lacing all over this country and he wants to get rich from them."

"How's he going to do that?"

"He's going to buy up lands where he thinks the rail lines will go. The partner said that soon these lands will officially become part of the Minnesota Territory, and then it all will become a state soon after. That means more settlers. To move settlers in, railroads will be needed. Logging will still be needed for building, but railroads will be where the big money will be. Buying and selling land is easier than setting up logging camps and sawmills."

"So, in the meantime, he uses his money to buy lands where the rail lines *might* go, and we'll have to make do with the little he gives us for food." Harry rubbed his chin again.

"Let's unload the sledge so you can see what we have. Whatever there is has to last all of this month and January, too."

The first thing Ellie noticed was there were no coffee beans, but lots of sacks of flour, oats, dried corn, beans, and peas. One small jug of molasses. A whole slaughtered pig. No sausages. No hams. Just a few gristly ham hocks.

"That's it?" Ellie's voice cracked.

"That's it. I bargained as much as I could, but I only could but the cheapest of everything."

"The men need meat to do hard work in the woods. And plenty more, too."

"Sorry. I'm as sick about it as you are. I even spent some of my own money on tobacco. Didn't dare come back and tell the men that we aren't getting any more. When I go back to Port Charles at the end of January, I probably won't be able to get any then with the meager allowance I get to spend. I quit using chewing tobacco when I was gone. It was hard at first day or two, but I think I can get through it." Axel threw a tin of tobacco on the table. "I don't know how we're going to divide that up."

CHAPTER 16

The loggers stamped their boots and shouted. Cuss words in every language flew about the room. *Merde! Voi paska! Dritt! Skit!* The men interrupted Axel with profanities as he told each bit of the bad news. *Djevel! Perkele!* "We work our arses off in the freezin' cold every day. How we gonna work if we don't have enough food? We just might as well get out of here and check out one of the other camps—one not owned by Mr. Woods."

"I know you work hard. Everyone here does. We're up and at it before daylight and still at it after dark. I'll bet that Mr. Woods hasn't done a lick of hard work in his life and doesn't care what you all do to make him rich. He holds the purse strings and can dole out the pennies anyway he wants." Axel looked at the small tin of tobacco he'd bought and shook his head.

"And what about our pay? How do we know he'll ever dig in those deep pockets of his?"

"Yeah, the thaw will come. We'll pack up to go home to our wives and families who'll be waiting and expecting us to have a pouch of money. The kids'll have outgrown their old shoes and be needin' new. And we won't have a stinkin' coin in our pockets."

"Yeah! What if he uses *our* money to buy railroad lands instead? The work will have been done. We can't take that back. He'll still have the logs we froze our butts off for. He can just turn his back on us. Sell the logs and use the money for more land."

"He should change his name from Mr. Woods to Mr. Railway or Mr. Iron Horse."

"That's not a bit funny. He might."

Big John and other men at his table muttered, "He's as bad as the *Wiindigoo*. No matter how much *Wiindigoo* eats, it's not enough. He wants more. No matter how much money Boss Woods makes, it's not enough. He wants more."

The complaints lasted the whole time Ahni filled bowls with bean soup, and Mam filled coffee mugs with the steaming brew.

"We even gonna have coffee after this batch runs out?"

"What we eatin' for the rest of the winter? Oatmeal and more oatmeal? Three times a day like I've heard that's all they get in some of the camps? Setting off for another camp isn't even such a good idea."

It wasn't the usual quiet supper time when the only sounds were the slurping of soup and the cling-clang of spoons against the tin bowls. When Ahni brought another plate of bread to the table with all her friends, Cloudy asked her, "Do you have a home to go back to? *Oosan* waiting for you at home? *Gookomis*?" Then he said the words so Ahni could understand. Father? Grandmother?

Ahni stammered a bit, not wanting to talk about Pap. She finally said "Pap and Grammy—my *Gookomis*—are at home. I hope they're . . ." What did she hope? That Grammy didn't have to work in the saloon just to get a bowl of stew at the end of the day? That Pap wasn't drinking himself into a wild rage while she, Mam, and Grammy worked hard? What was going to happen to her and Mam when the camp closed for the summer, and they had nowhere to go but home?

White Wolf saw Ahni's eyes tear up and her knees tremble. "Do not worry," he said. "They will be glad to have you with them again."

His words were kind, but Ahni wasn't sure Pap would be glad to see her again. He blamed her for Big Thunder's death. Big John had told her that being born during an eclipse was not a bad thing and that she hadn't caused Alfred to go missing. Even now, when some of the loggers listened to Axel tell all the bad news, they shot side-long looks at Ahni. *They were blaming her again! The girl who brought bad luck to the camp.*

It was a sleepless night for everyone. Ahni worried about everything. Pap, Grammy, the man she'd seen entwined in a tree, the *Wiindigoo*, *Nalka*, and most of all, Mam who seemed tired all the time. Ellie was doing more and more of Mam's work, so was Ahni. Even Harry. Harry. Ahni even worried about the nights that Mam stayed up late with Harry. She listened as hard as she could to hear what Harry was saying, but he spoke so low, she couldn't make out any of his words. Was Mam writing words on his hand to say what she wanted?

In the morning, when the loggers came in for breakfast, they didn't stomp their boots. They didn't talk at all, except for Kalle, Matti, and Asko who always said Good Morning in their own language. *Hyvää huomenta.* Ahni had learned to say that to them, too. Word had spread through the bunk house that Boss Man Woods didn't care at all for the loggers, but was buying land so he could build a railroad. Sven exaggerated everything he heard by claiming that no one would get paid and all they'd have to eat from now on were beans, peas, and oats.

Even the platters stacked high with freshly flipped flapjacks didn't liven the woods crew. Ahni had trouble smiling as she brought food to the tables. Cloudy noticed and softly whispered, "*Giiwedin-anong*, bring us some sun this gloomy morning." She smiled as she remembered when White Wolf had given her the name for the North Star. It was two days until Sunday. If there was time that day, she planned to ask if there was a story behind her Ojibwe name like there was for White Wolf's.

The mood was dark and heavy as the men picked up their noon sandwiches made of thick slabs of bread with thin slices of ham—the opposite of what they usually had been. Even when Axel stood at the door and offered a pinch of tobacco to everyone, it didn't brighten the mood of the men who were setting out for a long cold day sawing and chopping.

Ellie tried to cheer everyone as they cleared and washed the breakfast dishes. Axel blew out the candle lamps in the mess hall before Tarmo could sweep and mop the floor. "What?" Tarmo asked. "I need light to see what I'm doing!"

"I forgot to tell you and everyone else. I didn't have enough money for more candles. Food is more important than light. Tonight, I'll tell the loggers that whatever candles they have in the bunk house will have to do for the season unless Mr. Woods has a change of heart and finds some money hidden under his fancy feather mattress."

"I wouldn't want your job," Tarmo said. "One more piece of bad news piled on top of all the other. When the men go to bed with half empty stomachs, they would get some comfort in being able to see enough to play a game of cards. How'll they sharpen their saws with no light?"

"That I don't know. Maybe they'll all have to sit around one candle. The shortest, darkest days are still ahead. That's good and bad. Good because their days in the woods are shorter. Bad because they'll have to save every bit of candle possible."

Ahni thought about that. With no candle light, maybe Mam would come right to bed with her instead of staying up with Harry. Ahni hoped that was so.

CHAPTER 17

On Saturday, Harry took count of the food stores. He told Ellie and Mam, "We have enough flour, peas, beans, corn, and oats for the whole season even if we have to make more bread and flip more flapjacks to make up for less ham and sausages. Axel and Tarmo will help by bringing down deer during the week. They already have one hanging behind the bunk house. The men like venison stew."

"How about potatoes, carrots, rutabagas, cabbage, onions, pumpkin, and squash? Are we going to have enough of those?" Then Ellie added, "Apples and raisins?"

"We brought in enough potatoes and rutabagas for the whole season when we set up camp. We'll still have to keep count anyway. With less meat in the stew, we'll need more of the root vegetables. We're low on carrots, onion, and cabbages so just make thin slices of them for the soups and stews."

"Is there any good news?" asked Ellie.

"We'll be able to have pumpkin and squash pie once a week. And a few raisins mixed into the oatmeal. Not enough apples for pies. To make them last longer, you'll have to make watery sauce with thin slices."

That night, the kitchen crew sat in the dark after their work was done. Tarmo came in with Axel. They carried a bucket filled with fish.

"Glory be," Ellie jumped up so she could hug her husband.

Harry got up, too. "Tomorrow, we'll roast the pig Axel brought back with him. That should cut the grumbling at least for a day. We'll keep the fish frozen in a snow bank until Monday. Then we'll make a big fish stew. After that, we'll start using the venison. Sven won't be able to complain that it's bean or pea soup every night."

Ahni bent over the bucket counting the fish. "Just eight?"

"What do you mean? Just eight! We had to fight off about a hundred other fish that tried to jump into our bucket. They were begging for us to bring them to see you. Their exact words were, 'We hear you have a smart little girl in camp. Take us to see her. We want her to sink her wiggly teeth into us!'"

"They not say that an' not try jump in bucket," Ahni grinned a gap-toothed grin at Tarmo and wiggled another tooth for him to see. "And if they did, why you not bring more so we have lots in stew?"

"Have to let some fish stay in river so they'll make more fish. Then there'll be even more fish next time we go freezing our noses and toes catching them for you."

"You mean fish make baby fish?"

"Yup. Baby fish that grow into big fish."

"Like me. I was baby girl. Then I grew. I big girl now. Mam have baby in belly that grow and grow, too."

Everyone was stunned into silence. They looked at Mam, curious. Mam put her hands to her belly. She looked more puzzled than anyone else when she heard Ahni's words. She hadn't told her. She hadn't told anyone what she suspected.

"Is that right?" Ellie asked Mam as Harry, Axel, and Tarmo pretended the bucket of fish was very interesting.

Mam nodded and reached for Ahni's hand.

H-o-w y-o-u k-n-o-w?

Ahni looked bewildered, too. "Have baby in tummy?"

Mam nodded slowly. She spread her hands and shrugged her shoulders, asking Ahni again with her whole body how she knew.

"Just know. Nobody tole me. Maybe see baby in dream. You hole hands to tummy alla time when not be making bread. One day, I know. Maybe *Nalka* or *Wiindigoo* or some other beast whisper to me."

Mam hadn't told anyone. She'd puzzled how to tell. She'd worried that Harry would send her home. Here at the camp, Ahni was happy. She smiled and had plenty to eat. Even if they'd have to eat oatmeal every day, that was better than not eating anything. Besides, she herself liked Ellie and Tarmo and the way they teased each other. And she liked how kind Harry was. Now her secret was out. Even if Ahni hadn't said the words, the news would have been out soon enough. She ran her hand over her tummy feeling the soft mound that would grow month by month. She was certain that the baby would be born soon after the winter logging season was over. April or May. She'd be back home by then. Grammy would deliver the baby. Pap, well, she wasn't sure he would welcome another mouth to feed. She shivered and bit her lower lip thinking what he'd say and do.

Ellie took Mam by the hand and led her back to the little table in the corner. "This why you're so tired all the time?"

Mam nodded. Tears glistened in her eyes.

"Can you keep working at least another month or so?"

Mam squeezed Ellie's hand gently as she nodded again.

"Do you want to go home now or do you want to wait? I hope you don't want to go now. I don't know what we'd do without you and Ahni. If you need to go, I hope you leave Ahni here. She's a good helper. Tarmo and I love her and would take good care of her. Harry would, too."

Tears rolled down Mam's cheeks. Harry and Axel left to take the fish outside to bury in the snow, so Ahni sat by Mam. Tarmo carried the candle lantern from the kitchen with him as he sat, too. "I told Flora that when she needs to return home, you and I could keep Ahni here and care for her the rest of the season. She's such a good worker. No trouble at all."

Tarmo put a hand on Ahni's shoulder. "Ya, I'd like a good, smart daughter like you who's passed that burp and fill the diaper stage. Flora, don't you worry a bit. Whatever you decide, and whenever you need to leave, we'll make sure that it all works out the best for you."

Mam took Ahni's hand and wrote on it for a long time. Ahni wiggled her tooth as Mam wrote, then she told everyone, "Mam wants to know if you want to keep me for a daughter always or just for here at the camp when she has to leave?"

Tarmo and Ellie looked at each other. Ahni saw their eyes hold fast to each other. Then Ellie said, "Either way, we don't want Flora worrying about a new baby and what will happen to you. It's a long winter and two months or more before Flora has to start taking it easy. She's already tired most of the time even though the baby isn't showing much yet."

Harry and Axel came back in and sat at the nearby table. Mam looked at them, then wrote on Ahni's hand.

Ahni's shoulders slumped and tears slid from her eyes as she said to Harry, "Mam wants to know if you want us to leave tomorrow."

Harry put his hat and elbows on the table. His voice caught as he said, "Absolutely not! I know nothing about women having babies, but as long as she and Ellie tell me what's going on, and if it's safe for Flora to stay here, she's welcome. If she needs to rest, she rests. If she needs to eat, she eats. That goes for Ahni, too. I don't know what we'd do without the two of them here."

Mam reached over to hug Ahni, but she slipped from Mam's grasp and headed for the stables.

Sunday didn't belie its name. A bright sun shone; the sky was blue with a few fluffy clouds. The loggers were cheered by the brilliant weather, by being able to sleep later, and having time for a little bit of fun. When they started piling out of their bunks, they caught the aroma of roasting pork. Axel, Tarmo and Harry had already set the pig over the same pit they had dug for roasting venison. Fat dripped onto the hot embers and sizzled.

It was as though everyone knew that this was the last Sunday before the rationing of foods would start. The loggers pulled off their hats and let the full sun shine on their faces. To everyone's surprise, Axel brought out a squeeze box and played a lively polka. Ahni watched as his fingers flew from key to key without even looking.

"Show me!" Ahni fingered the bellows.

Axel slid the accordion straps from his shoulders, and held accordion while Ahni slipped her arms through the straps. "Oof! Heavy!"

"Let's wait until later when we go inside. Then you can sit, and it won't feel so heavy." Axel slid the straps back onto his own shoulders.

The day flew by as the loggers and kitchen crew washed their clothes, took steam baths, sharpened their axes and saws, and tapped their toes to the music. Some even danced in a circle while others ate their fill of juicy, roasted pork. Before the sun got too low in the sky, Matti called out, "Blanket toss!" Ahni smiled so wide that she showed her missing tooth as she jumped onto the middle of the blanket.

"Heave Ho!" the loggers called out as they lifted the blanket over their heads, lowered it, and then gave the big toss that sent Ahni soaring into the sky time and time again. When the men were all breathless, and Ahni was dizzy with delight, Espen called a stop to it saying, "Time for reading from the good book. Remember, Sunday not only day to wash stinky underwear, but to learn good lessons. Only two weeks before Christmas. We need to honor that."

A few of the men mumbled and suddenly remembered that they needed to be rub their boots with lard to keep them from becoming sopping wet in the snow. Others followed Espen into the mess hall. Ahni had liked the story about David and the giant Goliath so much that she followed Espen. She hoped Axel would remember to bring his accordion so she could learn to make music after Espen's story was over.

"... and Mary was with a child of the Holy Ghost ... And she shall bring forth a son and call his name Jesus ..." Ahni had been close to dozing as Espen had droned on and on about who begat whom in a long line of people with funny names, but when she heard the words *child* and *holey ghost*, she jerked fully awake. The holey ghost had brought Mary a child. She now knew how Mam had gotten a baby in her belly.

When she'd been tossed high on the blanket, she'd dared take a quick look at the tall spruce tree where she'd seen the mossy bearded man the first time she'd been tossed high into the skies. He wasn't there, but on the last toss after Espen had called for quits, she looked again. In an instant she thought she saw him swinging down from the branches. Later, after hearing Espen's story, she wondered if she'd seen the holey ghost and if he was there to check on the baby growing in Mam's belly.

After Espen closed his book and left for the bunk house, Cloudy and White Wolf stayed behind. "You want to hear Ojibwe story that's kind of like David and Goliath? At least it's about a little creature doing what all the big ones couldn't do."

"Tell me. I like David and Goliath story. Sometimes I feel so small I can't do anything. Like when Pap got mad an' yell an' hit. If I try an' stop him, he just slap me away like pesky mosquito. I want hear story of little one who so strong she overcome big an' mean."

Harry brought a pot of cedar tea and some mugs to the table. Tarmo set the one candle in the middle as Ellie and Flora came to hear the story, too.

Cloudy said, "Many people tell this story. Some tell it differently than what I say. I tell it as *Nookomis* told me. Important part is still the same." He nodded to Ahni, "When the story is over, you tell me what the important part is. The part I want you to remember."

"I listen every word," she promised wiggling a tooth.

"Long ago, before man came to live on earth, all the beasts of the forests could talk to each other. The bear bragged about how strong he was. The lynx bragged about how fast he was. The crow bragged about how smart he was. The other beasts got tired of hearing them boast of how strong, fast, and smart they were, so they declared that there would be a contest to determine what was best—strong, fast, or smart."

Ahni whispered, "What was contest?"

White Wolf whispered back, "Wait and listen. The best part is coming."

"I think bear wins. He big an' strong."

Mam tapped Ahni on the lips reminding her it was time to listen.

Cloudy sipped his tea, then went on. "The otter, eagle, and fox declared that whoever could snare the sun and keep it from rising in the morning would be the winner."

"'Easy,' growled the bear. 'Just as it begins to rise, I'll grab it in my arms and stuff it into a snare. Then I'll hold onto the rope so it can't move.'

"'Easy,' snarled the lynx. 'I'll just run as fast as I can before it rises. When I get to the spot where it peeks over the horizon, I'll spread my snare so when it tries to rise, it will be caught. As quick as a wink, I'll pull the snare tight and tie it to an oak tree, so the sun can't start its way across the sky.'

"'Easy,' cawed the crow. 'I'll just spread my black wings over the sun. It'll think it's still night and not time to wake up. While it's still sleeping, I'll spread the snare over it and not let it out.'

"For seven days the three of them tried out their plans. None worked until the eighth day when they finally decided to work together. The crow kept the sun sleeping. The lynx set the snare in just the right spot, and the bear grabbed the sun and stuffed it into the snare. Working together they dragged the sun into a huge cave. The bear, the lynx, and the crow called all the creatures of the forest together. 'We have captured the sun!' they declared. 'We all won!'"

"Good story," said Ahni. "Teaches us to work together."

"Story's not over," whispered White Wolf.

Ahni drank the rest of her tea, wiggled her tooth, and waited quietly for Cloudy to start again.

"With the sun snared and hidden in a cave, darkness covered the earth all day as well as all night. Soon all the creatures and people began to complain because it was dark and cold all the time. The squirrel told the bear, 'What's so good about being the strongest if we're cold and in the dark all the time?'

"The fisher told the lynx, 'What's so good about being fast if we're in the dark and cold all the time?' And the chickadee told the crow, 'What's so good about being the smartest if we're cold and in the dark all the time?'

"The bear, the fox, and the crow met behind an old oak tree. They knew their bragging days were over. They didn't like the cold and dark either, so they decided to have a new contest. Whoever could free the sun from its snare so that it rose and gave warmth and light would be the winner.

"The lynx ran the fastest so he got to the cave where the sun was hidden first. He tried and tried, but he couldn't untie the cords of the snare. The bear tried next. He tore at the snare with his claws. He pulled so hard, he broke most of his claws, but the snare held fast. Soon he had to give up, too. The crow swooped down and pecked at the snare. It didn't give. He couldn't as much as break one thin cord."

The corners of Ahni's mouth drooped. "Ohh, nooooo!"

"Not the end yet. Keep listening," White Wolf reminded her again.

"Meanwhile, a little chipmunk watched. When the three shook their heads and gave up, the chipmunk started to gnaw at the cords. He gnawed and gnawed for long time. One day, one cord snapped free. Another, the next day. Finally, the whole snare broke loose, the sun rolled out of the cave and rose to warm the land."

"Chipmunk freed sun! Not big strong bear. Not fast lynx. Not smart crow. But little teensy chipmunk! Just like little David! That important part. That part I'll always remember. Sometimes, the little do what big strong, fast, and smart can't." Ahni snuggled up to her mother and wiggled her tooth. Sundays were her favorite day. Bath. Not so much work. Good food. Blanket toss. Story about a holey ghost giving mothers a baby. Story of how little chipmunk could do what nobody else could.

CHAPTER 19

The next two weeks were hard on everyone. Harry counted out each slice of ham, each carrot, each scoop of coffee. A sharp wind blew relentlessly out of the north. Reino and the men who worked in the woods felt the bitter wind every minute. They spread lard on their faces to keep their cheeks, chins, and noses from freezing. Deep in the woods, they heaped branches from the fallen trees and lit the piles to build fires to warm themselves.

On the day Ellie crossed December 23 from her calendar, she said, "Sunday tomorrow. Anyone notice the days getting longer?"

"Ask me again in about a month," Reino grumbled.

"We need to do something special tomorrow," she added. "Not only days getting longer, but Espen will want to read about the baby born in the manger and the wise men. We should all take time to listen to him at least this once."

"Hopefully the weather will be sunny and warm so we can spend time outside without freezing." Tarmo washed a big kettle while Ellie and Ahni measured ingredients for the morning's flapjacks.

"I have a bag full of something good that everyone will get tomorrow." Harry patted Ahni on the head as he said that.

"Liver an' heart an' onions?" she asked.

"As good as liver, heart, and onions. Besides that, remember when I told you that we'd have a cake when your two wiggly teeth fell out?"

"Ya! I pulled second one this morning. It wiggled so much it 'bout fell out all by itself. An' tomorrow Axel say he gonna teach me more 'cordion music."

"If we have time, we'll even get everyone dancing around the bonfire. But for now, let's all get some sleep. I have to get up early to make and bake cake. Flora, do you want to help me?"

Ahni woke early on Sunday morning. All night she'd wondered what the "something good" that Harry had said everyone would get. She hoped it would be a stick of peppermint candy. In the old days, before Big Thunder died, Pap used to buy a bag of those. He'd pass them out at the big solstice celebration. That was when everyone in their little settlement turned out for a huge crackling bonfire in the dark of night. Even young children stayed up late dancing while someone played a fiddle, and others blew their willow whistles or tapped on homemade drums.

Ahni reached to wake Mam, but her straw-stuffed bed was already empty. Harry was up, too. She heard him clattering bowls, mixing, and stirring. *The cake to celebrate her missing teeth!* Ahni scrambled up and ran her fingers through her hair. As she pulled her boots on, she heard Harry say, "Ahni, your cake is ready to go into the oven. If you want to see it before it bakes, you'd better get up."

Mam reached out to hug Ahni as she scooted to look. There wasn't one cake pan, but three. "Enough cake for everyone, not just the tooth-missing girl." Harry picked Ahni up and swirled her in a circle just like Tarmo always did.

"What cake taste like?" Ahni asked.

"Well, I chopped up some old wrinkled pickles and put them in for spice. I thought apple stems and cores might add crunch. Tarmo gave me some horse hair to add for bulk. Oh, this'll be a yummy cake."

"No tease me! What really taste like?"

"You'll have to wait until it's baked to find that out," Harry said as he slid the pans into the oven. "But a hint is, no apple cores, but the best part of the apple, along with some raisins, and brown sugar to sweeten it for a sweet girl."

"Apple raisin cake. Never had afore, but sounds good."

Ahni and Mam bathed in one of the steam huts early. They hoped their hair would dry fast as they sat by the big wood stove. The loggers were in their Sunday-best moods as they took turns watching the deer roast while others washed their clothes and steamed themselves clean of any itches. Others sharpened their axes and saws. When the venison finished roasting along with potatoes and squash that Harry had buried under the hot embers, Espen gathered everyone and said, "Tonight is Christmas Eve, so we celebrate the birth of the Baby Jesus this day, even though tomorrow we'll be back in the woods. So, before we eat, I'll read his story."

Some of the men groaned, murmuring, "Why can't we just eat and celebrate later?"

Espen cleared his throat as he turned pages to his book mark. "... shepherds saw a great star in the skies ... and angels came to them singing that a king was born ... and the baby wrapped in swaddling clothes will be found lying in a manger ..."

"What's a manger?" whispered Ahni.

Tarmo whispered back, "It's a stable, like where we keep our horses. It has lots of nice soft hay for a baby to lie on."

"Mam gonna have baby in stable?"

"Shhh. Listen," said Ellie.

Espen had been reading all the while, "... three wise men came from afar carrying gifts ... King Herod gave orders to kill baby Jesus ..."

"Scary story. I no like. Bad man wantin' to kill Baby Jeez. Baby too little to hurt big man like David did to Goliath."

Mam held Ahni close to herself so she wouldn't interrupt again. Ahni only half-listened as Espen read more. She softly pressed her hand against Mam's tummy and thought about the baby in there brought by a holey ghost. She knew about ghosts. Pap had told many stories, but never about one with holes. She wondered how it had gotten holes in it.

When Espen finished his story, Ahni said, "I glad that the bad men didn't get to kill Baby Jeez. Good thing angels came outta sky an' tole his mam and pap to flee to that place called 'gypt where they'd be safe." She thought about the man she'd seen in the tree. Maybe he was an angel who came to make sure the baby was safe in her mother's tummy, "Mam, where we go if baby from holey ghost not safe?"

Mam held Ahni's hand and wrote on it. N-o w-o-r-r-y. Then slid her arm around her daughter. Ellie smiled to see the two of them cuddled together as mother and daughter. She wished again, as she had for many years, for a daughter of her own.

The rest of the day was as good as Ahni had hoped. Axel taught her to play the alphabet song on his accordion. Ahni had already learned to sing it when her Grammy had taught her the alphabet, so she sang as she pulled then pushed the bellows open and shut and fingered the keys. Later in the day, when the sun sank below the trees, and the cooking fire was glowing embers, Axel said, "Let's go inside to keep warm."

As everyone settled at the tables, he began playing a soft melody. Ahni watched as he worked the bellows and wondered in awe that he didn't even have to look at his fingers as they picked out the melody. He and others began to sing, "Silent night. Holy night. All is calm . . ." When they were finished singing and bowed their heads, Espen asked him to play it again. Then, he and the Norwegian loggers sang in their language. *"Glade jul. Hellige jul! Engler daler ned i skjul."*

Kalle and Matti asked for him to play the melody yet again as the Finns sang. *Jouluyö, juhlayö!*

The Swedes took their turn, too. *"Stilla natt, heilga natt! Allt är frid."*

When Axel put his accordion away, the loggers sat silently, each lost in his own thoughts. Ahni looked from man to man wondering about the melody and the words that had changed everyone from laughter and joking to such a deep quiet that the only sound was of a log spitting in the barrel stove that warmed the mess hall.

Ahni was eager for Harry to cut the cakes he and Mam had made, and she was even more eager to learn what Harry had hidden away for everyone. She tried not to wiggle as all the men sat quietly, but the quiet lasted longer than she had patience for.

"Cake time, yet?" she called to Harry.

The men raised their heads and laughed. "Cake?" White Wolf asked. The silence had been broken. Harry, Mam, and Ellie hurried to cut cake while Ahni brought plates to the men. Tarmo carried the gallon pots of coffee to the tables. "Drink your fill," he told the men. "Not much of it left." While everyone ate and drank, Harry came out with a gunny sack that bulged with his promise of "something good."

"Ahni, come and pass out the real surprise."

"What it be?" she asked.

"Reach in and find out."

Ahni did and pulled out a handful of oddly shaped brown things. "Ugly," she said. "What they?"

"Peanuts! Ugly to look at, but wait until you taste them!"

Tarmo took the bag from Ahni and poured piles of peanuts on each table. Following the lead of Cloudy and the others, Ahni took one, cracked it open, and popped the little nut into her mouth. At first, she didn't like the peanut, but as she chewed and it mushed in her mouth, she discovered a mealy taste unlike any she'd had before. Soon she was reaching for a whole handful like the men were.

As she snuggled on her straw-filled bed that night, she thought that Christmas Eve Sundays were the best Sundays of all.

CHAPTER 20

Sunday was over. Christmas day was just like every other work day. The loggers rose before the sun, ate, and headed out for a day in the woods while the cook shack crew cleaned, mixed bread dough, and set the beans and ham hocks into two huge pots. One for the noon meal and the other for evening.

When the sun was high in the sky, Axel brought his horse around to the cook shack. Ellie and Flora carried sacks with tin bowls, spoons, and loaves of hot bread to the sleigh. Harry loaded a big soup cauldron next to the sacks. The two men *Gee-upped* the horse and headed to where the loggers worked. No ham and sausages for sandwiches meant that every day from now on, they would have to bring soup to the logging site for the men's mid-day meal. This meant more work for the cook crew. They'd have dishes to wash and the big cauldron to scrub when Harry and Axel returned. Daily trips to the logging site also took away Axel's time from hunting with Tarmo.

Sven recognized the cauldron as one of the huge kettles in which they heated water on Sundays and swished their clothes around in to wash. "Might as well have just left my sweaty socks in the dirty water yesterday, then at least we'd have more to chew on today."

He laughed, but none of the other men did. Times were hard and getting harder. The days were still short and cold. Espen reminded them daily that the days would be getting longer. More daylight would return day by day. "Just like when Jesus was born bringing light to the world." The men didn't care if it was Jesus' birth that brought light to the world or if was a chipmunk chewing the cords to free the sun. Christmas and the solstice were over. They looked forward to and also dreaded the longer and warmer days that meant longer hours in the woods.

As cheerful as everyone in the cook shack had been the day before, they were just as quiet and gloomy that day. Ellie didn't smile. When Tarmo came in for his noon meal, he didn't take Ahni by the hands and swing her around. When Harry returned from delivering the noon soup, his nose and cheeks were beet red. "Don't know how the men can stand it for hours every day," he said as he wiped his nose. Axel came in, slurped a bowl of soup, and left without saying a word. Even Mam didn't pull Ahni to her side and brush hair from her eyes as she usually did at least three times a day.

It didn't get any better when the loggers returned at night scraping snow off their boots and plopping down on their benches. They mumbled, "Cursed cold!" as they pulled out red pocket rags to wipe their sniffling noses.

Even the men at Ahni's favorite table ducked their heads to gulp bowl after bowl of pea soup. Then they wiped their bowls clean with chunks of the freshly baked bread and left for their bunks. Mam tried her best to help with the dishes and cleaning, but she was slow so Ahni helped more than usual. No matter how busy they were, or how late the night got, Harry insisted that no crumbs were left under a table and every spill was wiped up with a clean rag.

The whole week crept by as everyone had more work and less solid food. On pea soup days, it was for both noon and night. The same on bean soup days. There was noticeably less ham and fewer sausages on the fry skillets and in the cooking kettle. The loggers huddled close to the barrel stove and gobbled their soup as fast as they could before leaving for a night of sharpening axes and jumping into bed.

The following Sunday according to Ellie's calendar, was the last day of the year. There was no deer to roast over the outdoor fire. The sun didn't even bother peeking out from behind the cloudy sky. A stiff wind blew out of the north rattling the door to the cook shack. It was so cold that Ahni and Mam didn't take their turn in the steam bath hut. When Ahni asked why, Mam wrote on Ahni's hand that it was too cold to dry their hair. The loggers huddled around the stove, not leaving a single spot for Ahni to squeeze in between Cloudy and White Wolf.

She spent the day in the kitchen keeping as close as she could to the wood-fired cook stove. She watched Harry reach for a clay jar from the shelf above the stove, measure out some bubbly mixture from the jar and put it into a bread bowl. Then he added flour and water to the clay jar. "What that ugly, bubbly, gray stuff be?" she asked.

"That," Harry said as he set the clay jar back onto the high shelf, "is probably the most important thing in this cook shack. Ugly or not, we wouldn't have bread or flapjacks without it."

"Huh? I no unnerstand."

Harry took the clay jar down from the shelf again. "Look. This is the starter that makes bread and flapjacks fluffy and yummy. Every time I take some out to use, I add more flour and water to feed it and keep it growing for next time."

"Feed it?"

"Ya, just like you and me, it needs to be fed so it'll stay alive and grow."

"It living thing? Even with no legs an' eyes like animal? No leaves like a tree?"

"It is. See all the bubbles. That shows that it's alive and growing. I have to keep it warm so it won't die. If that happens, it'll take me at least a week to get a new batch growing. No one would like the hard bread I'd be making during that time."

"Teach me how."

"All righty. From now on you'll be my helper when it comes to make sour dough starter."

"I learn lots here. How play accordion. How clean tables an' floor. How chop apples for pies. Now, how make starter for bread an' flapjacks. Oh, an' I know about days an' months from Ellie's calendar. An' stories about little David an' baby Jeez."

"We need to teach you your numbers, too. How to add and subtract." Tarmo had been listening. "Eight years old. You're old enough to learn lots more so we need to start some lessons during this long winter."

"Look here," Ellie said pointing to her calendar. "It's the last day. December 31. Tomorrow I'll put up a new calendar showing all the months of 1849—a new year. Let's hope it'll be better than this last."

Harry, Ellie, and Tarmo began teaching Ahni how to count, add, and subtract. "Ahni, how many apples are in this bowl? And now? If I take five out for a pie, how may are left? How many apples do I need if I make eight pies with five apples in each?"

Ahni needed to count on her fingers for that answer. "Forty!" she exclaimed.

Harry couldn't turn around without Ahni asking, "Time to feed sour dough? Bread high enough to bake? How many potatoes for bean soup? Why my butt make music when I eat beans? And I smell stinky? Mam, too? How many peas in soup? Carrots? Rutabagas? Why cabbages all brown an' yucky?"

The cabbages were all brown and slimy. They'd frozen and didn't look fit to be eaten. Not even chopped small into soup. The weather had turned so cold that the food storage was colder than Harry wanted it to be. Ellie and Mam helped lug the sacks of root vegetables, pumpkins, squash, and apples into a far corner of the mess hall so they wouldn't freeze, too.

"Ugly," Ahni said when she saw the gunny sacks piled in a corner.

"Ugly, ya, but we have to keep watch on them too. If that corner gets too cold, we have to move them closer to the barrel stove," said Harry.

"What happen if they get too cold?"

"If the potatoes freeze, they don't taste good. Maybe we couldn't use them at all. Then, we'd be down to real bean and pea soup. The loggers wouldn't like that. Me neither."

"I watch them. Look ever day an' make sure they not get too cold," Ahni shivered a bit just thinking of bean soup without any carrots or potatoes. And no apple pie.

The new year came in on a blast of cold air and sunless days that lasted the whole month of January. One day, Axel's thermometer read below zero. He took it down from the outside wall of the cookshack the morning it read -35 degrees. He didn't want the men to see how cold it was. They'd balk at having to go out into the woods when it was that cold. He told Harry to set out the crock of lard so the men could smear it on their faces in hopes of preventing frost bite. Harry said, "The lard is even running low. We need it for flapjacks and bread. This camp doesn't run on empty stomachs. Maybe the men should stay out of the cold on days like this."

Axel shrugged. "We've got a big dilemma here. Boss Man Woods wants thousands of logs to feed his mill come spring. Logs are money to him. We need to keep the men fed and healthy. We need lard for baking. The men need it to protect their skin from the cold, but, you're right, I'm not so sure that lard will even work for a full day in weather like this."

"It's your call. Stay in camp on these frigid days. Healthy men. No frost bite. Or go work in the woods and risk frozen feet and faces while using up all the lard I need for cooking and baking."

"You're right, again. The answer is simple. I'll put the thermometer back up, and we all stay sheltered in camp any day it's -10 or below. Especially if there's a wind like today."

Reino the woods boss said, "Whew! I'm glad to hear that. A couple of the men already have frozen toes. We have to keep an eye on those. I hope they don't turn black. Then there'll be trouble."

Axel and Reino gathered a couple of men to cut cedar boughs for tea. Harry explained, "We're about to have the men in camp all day. Gotta keep the big coffee pots full of water heating for tea. And we'll need a few men to add more logs to the wood piles. Looks like we'll be heating the mess hall all day."

The blustery wind and sub-zero temperatures lasted several days. Tempers and patience grew short as the loggers grew bored. Axel and Harry tried to keep them busy by assigning each man to a group with tasks to do each day. One kept the wood piles stocked; a second gathered cedar for tea and kept the fires going under the cauldron to melt snow on the barrel heater in the bunk house, and yet another group fed the fires in the cook shack and mess. When the shallow well pump froze, they all had to pitch in carrying in snow to melt for cooking and washing. The chores and only two decks of cards were not enough to keep the men busy so they devised contests of arms and leg wrestling. No fights broke out because Axel sternly broke up the first sign of a scuffle by saying that anyone caught fighting would miss their next meal. The idle men also vied to see who could tell the tallest tale about the fabled logger Paul Bunyan, but they tired of that soon, too.

Axel brought out his squeeze box and offered to teach anyone who wanted to play. Asko and Matti taught Ahni a finger and string game they called Cat's Cradle. After the third day, loggers were ducking her invitations to play by saying that their fingers were too sore. Espen got on everyone's nerves by reading aloud from his book before and after each meal. Nobody was interested in who begat who hundreds of years ago.

Harry and the cook crew were as busy as ever. The loggers still ate stacks of flapjacks for breakfast. Huge kettles of pea or bean soup bubbled on the wood-fired stove. Cauldrons of snow melted on the barrel stove in the mess hall throughout the day. Ellie, Flora, and Ahni made bread and peeled mountains potatoes, carrots, and rutabagas.

And then the day came when Axel announced that the pinches of tobacco he passed out that day would be the last until the end of the month when he'd go to Port Charles again. That was, if the weather warmed. Two days later, Harry roasted the last of the coffee beans. The only ham he had for the pea soup were two ham hocks with mostly fat and gristle and little meat. The men began to grumble. First, they blamed the cheapskate Mr. Woods. Then some men began to eye Ahni and mutter.

"Her fault. She was born during an eclipse! Born bad!"

"This horrific weather! And what about Alfred? Where did he go? Did she have something to do with that?"

"She said she saw a man in the tree the same day Alfred went missing."

"Maybe she saw *Wiindigoo*."

"Is *Wiindigoo* real?"

"How long is this cold spell going to last? The cabbages even froze and are rotten! What trouble is that eclipse girl bringing next?"

Ahni got shivers when she heard the men talking and blaming her for everything. She complained while snuggling up to Mam. "I not bad. Didn't make weather bad or anything else!"

White Wolf tried to quell the murmurs about Ahni. "She's just a flesh and blood girl. She doesn't bring storms. She had nothing to do with Alfred. Or the cabbages. Or cheap Mr. Woods."

Harry even stepped in on the seventh day of the blustery freezing weather. "We've had cold spells before, and we'll have them again. Quit blaming Ahni! The wind is from the north. It's probably an Artic blast right out of the North Pole." He shook his head and murmured to Tarmo and Ellie, "I can't wait for a break in this weather so these guys will be back in the woods instead of sitting around here complaining and starting trouble."

The break came two days later when Axel's thermometer read minus ten before the sun was even up. Better yet, when the sun broke through the clouds, it warmed all the way up to zero. It was a relief for the cook crew as well as the loggers as they set out for the woods at last.

CHAPTER 21

The weather held—nippy cold—but not dangerously so. Ellie marked days off her calendar. "What month next?" Ahni asked when there were only two days not crossed off January and Axel started planning his trip to Port Charles. Ahni tried luring him into a game of Cat's Cradle by tying the string around his fingers as he tried to write a list of supplies that he hoped Mr. Woods had left enough credit for. "Bring something good. Peanuts or candy," she begged. Then she stopped. An image flashed in her head.

Not an image of the man in the tree, but of one of the loggers lying on the ground. An axe stuck in his leg. Red blood pooled in the white snow. Her heart lunged. She couldn't see who the man was, but hoped it wasn't White Wolf or one of the others she liked. She shook her head and tried to get rid of the vision, but it was too strong. A whisper brushed her ear. *Jalmer.* She tried to block the image and held her fingers to her ears. She hoped it wasn't Jalmer. She hoped it wasn't anyone. She hoped the men wouldn't look at her, blaming her. Whispering *Born Bad.*

Mam pulled Ahni away from the two men so they could finish the food list. Mam wove the string between her own fingers to start the game. Ahni snagged the string with her little fingers. The image of the bleeding man was still strong. She shook her head and tried to concentrate on the strings. The image faded. Her voice shook as she said, "Let's make Witch's Broom and then Cat's Whiskers." Those were the only two tricks she'd been able to make so far without knotting the string. With Ellie giving directions and Mam holding the string, she hoped to learn Jacob's Ladder next.

Still feeling jittery from seeing the flashing image and wanting to tell what she'd seen, Ahni whispered to Mam, "Jalmer's leg all chopped up."

Mam crinkled her forehead and signed to Ahni to say that again. She whispered. "Axe chop Jalmer's leg."

Ellie overheard, "What? What did you say?"

Ahni drooped her head.

"Tell me what you said about Jalmer," Ellie's looked concerned.

"Nothing. I just make things up." Ahni choked out the words.

"Just tell me. Something about Jalmer's leg?"

Ahni looked at Mam who twisted her fingers together and shook her head. Ahni tried to pull the right strings to make the Witch's Broom, but Mam dropped all the strings. Ahni picked them up. Everything was knotted. She tried to straighten the string, but the knots were too tight. She'd never get them right again. Maybe nothing would be right again.

Ellie's forehead furrowed and her lips were tight. She clutched Ahni's shoulder as she asked again, "What did you say about Jalmer's leg?"

Ahni wanted the string to unknot. She wanted Mam to play Cat's Cradle with her. She wanted Ellie to smile. She wanted her to let go of her shoulder. She yanked the string into one big knot and scowled, "Chopped up. Jalmer leg got axe in it."

Ellie let go of Ahni's shoulder, but she didn't smile.

Harry and Axel had been busy making their list so they hadn't heard what Ahni said. She was glad of that and listened as Harry called out, "Ham and smoked sausages are most important. If we get another cold spell or a big snow storm, you and Tarmo won't be able to go out hunting, so we'll need meat. Coffee beans will improve the moods of most of the men. They're not fond of the cedar tea I make when the coffee runs low. Dried peas and beans. We've had to double up using those, so won't make it through the next two months without more. Molasses. Raisins. We've got enough flour. If you can find corn meal, that would be good for a change. If you can't get hams, get more oats." He groaned. "I don't know what would happen if we ran out of oats. A couple pails of lard, too. That's about it."

"That's a plenty long list if Boss Woods is still penny pinching to save for his railroad."

Harry slammed a kettle on the table. "Remind him that rails are built on ties and the ties are made of wood and the wood comes from trees that are felled by lumberjacks and lumberjacks need to eat!"

Axel laughed. He'd never seen Harry so worked up, but knew he was right. Boss Woods might be planning to get rich from the railroads, but he still needed the logging camps. "I'll talk to Tarmo, too, see if there's anything he needs for the horses."

"And if you ask the men, they'll say *snus* and coffee."

"*Snus?* Is that what they're calling chewing tobacco these days?"

"Ya. Say it keeps their hearts beating in this cold weather."

"I know. I'd take a chaw of tobacco myself right now if I had it."

They were interrupted by the sound of a sledge grinding its way over the crusted snow. Ahni ran outside wanting to see and not wanting to see at the same time. Reino *whoa-ed* one of the logging horses to a stop by the cook shack, hopped off the small sledge, and yelled, "Get Axel and Harry out here to help. Tarmo, too."

Lying on the sledge was Jalmer. His leg was wrapped in a towel soaked with blood. A stinging bitterness surged from Ahni's stomach into her throat. She leaned over and threw up into the snow.

Axel pulled off his belt and wrapped it tightly around Jalmer's thigh. The man just lay there. "How long he's been bleeding like this?" he asked Reino.

"We got him on the sledge right away. I tried to put a belt around his leg, too, but he was yelling so loudly and fighting me so I just got here as fast as I could. He's as white as can be!"

"Probably shock and blood loss. I need to get a look at his wound. Hopefully we can stop the bleeding so I can sew it up."

CHAPTER 22

Deep inside herself, Ahni felt a sickly churning. She hadn't been in the woods, but she'd seen the axe bite into Jalmer's leg. She'd seen the blood. Axel was looking at her as if she'd done something wrong. As if *she* caused that axe to chop into Jalmer's leg instead of the tree. She knew that wasn't possible. She knew she hadn't caused it, but her whole insides churned with guilt. Her head ached.

Big John and Cloudy came rushing out of the woods as Axel wrapped blankets around Jalmer for the long wagon trip to Port Charles. Cloudy reached under his shirt and pulled out a pouch.

"Medicine for Jalmer," Big John said as he pulled a pouch out of his own shirt, too.

"You two need to get back to the crews chopping wood," Axel said impatiently.

"My medicine can stop bleeding." Big John offered his pouch again. "Dab a thick layer over the wound. The bleeding will stop."

"Well, I'll be. I've heard you Ojibwe have medicine for everything. Medicine you find in the woods. Leaves and roots of plants. You say it stops bleeding?"

Cloudy opened his pouch, "And here is powdered root. Mix a bit with water—even melted snow—to ease his pain. Use it now. Take both medicines with you."

Axel looked a little bit hesitant, but he unwrapped Jalmer's leg. Despite the belt that was supposed to stop the blood flow, the wound still seeped. Mam grasped Ahni's shoulder and tried to pull her away from watching, but Ahni shook her mother's hand off and watched as Cloudy sprinkled the powder onto some snow and then scooped it up for Jalmer to swallow. Big John dabbed his powder on the gaping wound while he chanted a few words in his language. Ahni wished she knew what he was saying. A few short moments after Big John spread his powder on Jalmer's leg, the blood began to clot.

Axel heaved a sigh of relief. "It's working. Maybe we'll save him and his leg after all."

"Don't forget to loosen that belt every once in a while," Ellie said, or it will cause more trouble than you already have."

"It'll slow you down, but the rough going will probably start the bleeding again. Put more powder on if that happens." Big John clasped Jalmer on the shoulder. "You're going to be all right. It'll hurt a lot, but you will heal."

Axel re-wrapped Jalmer in blankets and pocketed the list of foods and other supplies they'd need. After checking the horse and all the riggings, he said, "Off to Port Charles. Let's hope there's a doctor or someone who can fix Jalmer's leg so he can get back to work again."

It was quiet in the cook shack. Reino had headed back to the woods with Big John and Cloudy. Ahni peeled potatoes and hoped with all her might that Jalmer's leg would heal, and that she wouldn't be blamed because she was born bad. Harry chucked more wood into the big cook stove. He knew Axel would be gone for several days finding help for Jalmer and getting the supplies they'd need. He hoped Boss Man Woods had left a good-sized allotment for food. He hoped Jalmer would return ready to work. He shook his head, afraid neither of his hopes would come true.

Ellie and Flora had worry lines creasing their foreheads, too. Ellie kneaded a huge dough for bread. Her arms ached. She looked at Flora who struggled to pour beans from a big bag into the soup kettle. She should help, but how long could she keep helping Flora and still get her own job done? She watched Ahni peel potatoes. Peels curled and slid into a pile.

Ahni had gotten used to handling the little knife while peeling potatoes and apples. She stopped and looked at the blade. Then she held out one finger and poked the point of the knife into the tip of her finger making it bleed. She watched a drop of blood bead. Then she licked the drop off and squeezed her finger until another bright red drop arose. She stuck her whole finger into her mouth and sucked the salty blood away.

Ellie watched as Ahni cut herself and bled. She relaxed a bit when Ahni picked up another potato and started peeling again. She wondered why Ahni had purposely made her own finger bleed. How had she known that Jalmer's leg had gotten gashed by an axe? How could that girl possibly know something like that ahead of time? Could there really be something to her being born during an eclipse? Could a person actually be born bad? She slapped the dough she'd been kneading. She smacked it so hard that Harry looked up at her.

When the men returned from the woods that evening, Espen brought his black book with him. He held it close to his chest, over his heart. Sven spit into the wood pile as he walked past Ahni and held up two crossed fingers when he looked at her. Ellie groaned to herself when she saw that and hoped Flora didn't see. Trouble was brewing for the little girl, and she didn't deserve it.

The men ate quickly and quietly as usual, but it didn't seem usual to Ahni. A black mist seemed to hover over the whole mess area. When she brought bread to tables, the loggers didn't even look up. The pots of hot tea did not empty and require refilling like when there was coffee in the pots. Ahni fretted when Kalle and White Wolf didn't even give her friendly smiles when she brought bowls of apple sauce at the end of the meal.

As the men left the mess hall, Ahni watched the black mist leave with them. She thought they must be sad and worried about Jalmer. Then she remembered when Big Thunder had died. Little as she'd been, she'd seen the black mist settle over Pap and it had never seemed to leave as he sank further and further into drunken rages. She hoped the loggers wouldn't turn mean like Pap had. Besides, Jalmer hadn't died. She felt a beat of hope. Axel would bring Jalmer back when he returned with a wagon full of hams and bacon and other good things to eat. She held onto that hope and tried to envision it as real as she swabbed the tables and swept the floor.

When she'd finished cleaning the mess hall, she dragged a little stool to the tin sink. Harry poured warm water into it and into a rinse bucket. Ahni plunged her hands into the sudsy water and began washing and rinsing dishes. Mam helped by pulling the rinsed plates out and standing them on end in a wooden rack Harry had made. Meanwhile, Ellie measured flour for the morning's flapjacks and Harry tended to the sour dough starter.

No one said a word until Tarmo came in from tending to the horses. "Anything I can do to help? The horses are fed and watered. I shoveled the gutters clean as can be."

Ahni hoped he'd pick her up and swing her around like he usually did, but instead he helped Ellie carry a sack of flour back into the store room.

Harry was the next to speak. "Have you talked to Reino? How's he going to work with one less man?"

"Told me one team will be short a man, but that he'll join that team whenever needed. The work will be slower. And everyone has to be twice as careful. It's dangerous work out there." Tarmo scratched his head, glanced at Ahni and said, "That Espen says we need to cast out evil in the woods every day before starting work. He's upsetting some of the men by telling them things like 'Flee from evil now' and 'Deliver yourself from the wicked.' I guess he even went about in the bunkhouse muttering, 'Let no evil befall us this night.'"

"I know what you mean. He told me that he wanted to exorcise the mess hall. I didn't know what he meant so he explained that he needed to cleanse it of all bad spirits and cure the evil one who had invited the spirits in. I told him that the mess was for eating and eating only because we all had to get on with what we needed to do for the next day."

"He's always wanting to lead a revival here at the camp or a Sunday-go-meeting. He needs to find a preacher's job and not a logging job. He's going to cause a lot of trouble before the spring thaw comes when we can get out of here and back to our farms and families or whatever else there is that we do." Ellie shaped the bread dough into round loaves and set them to rise as she spoke.

"Let's just hope that Axel finds help for Jalmer and loads the wagon with all the goods we need for the next two or three months," Harry said. "I, for one, am hoping for an early thaw. I'll be taking the wanigan down the river on the log drive. Riding and cooking on the wanigan raft is dangerous enough. I'm glad I'm not one of the guys who run along the floating logs and break up jams with long poles during the high waters of a thaw. Those men have to be fearless."

"Fearless isn't enough. You gotta be half-nuts to ride the logs down the river like that. I've seen them break up jams. In the old country, I saw guys fall and never come up out of the water again. Plenty of them die." Tarmo's chin quivered as he talked. "My uncle was one of them. They found him downstream. Unrecognizable except for his clothes. Battered and torn by logs and river rocks when the swift current swept him away."

He paused for a moment, looked at Ellie and said, "Maybe we should get serious about getting on a wagon train headed to California. Plenty of excitement and danger, but nothing like this."

Ahni had been listening to every word. "What mean *wanigan* and *log drive?*" she finally asked. She wanted to know what Harry would be going down the river on.

"Wanigan," Harry began, "is a big raft made of logs lashed together. And they have to be lashed good otherwise they'll break up in rough water. That wouldn't be good. On the log raft is a little shack. That's my cook shack. The men on the log drive need plenty of good food. How much depends on how far the logging camp is upriver from the nearest sawmill. The men who ride the logs and break up log jams sleep on the wanigan at night, too. Some people call the log drivers *river pigs* or *river hogs*. I have no idea where those names came from."

"That what you call 'em, too?"

"Nope, I just call them crazy log drivers. Lucky we have men willing to risk their lives to do that. It has to be done or the log jams would never break up. Just get bigger and bigger."

"Do Mam an' I go on wanigan an' log drive, too?"

Instead of answering, Harry got busy clanging pans together, but he took a moment to take a quick glance at Flora who looked at Ahni. Ahni looked at Harry, then at Mam. Ahni knew then without being told that Harry and Mam had secrets. Secrets Ahni wanted to know.

Twelve days went by. Axel hadn't returned. Harry, Tarmo, and Reino paced nervously wondering what was keeping him.

"Maybe the trails are bad."

"Maybe his horse slipped and broke a leg."

"Don't even think things like that. We don't need any more troubles." Harry glanced at Ahni.

She piped up, "Maybe wagon heaping full of good things. Horse walk slow to pull such big load. Ham an' sausages. Coffee. Peanuts. Maybe even something sweet, even a sugar lump."

The men laughed. Not real laughs, but forced laughs. Harry scratched his chin as he looked at Ahni again.

Ellie wrinkled her forehead and said, "The men are tired of having to eat bean or pea soup without sausages or ham for every meal."

Tarmo rubbed his brow and said, "I'll get out in the woods every day after the teams leave and try to track down a deer. With this warmer weather, they'll be moving around looking to browse off cedar trees and whatever else they can reach. It won't be easy. They'll be far from the logging area. Hopefully the snow in the woods won't be too deep for me to trudge through."

"Worse part of it is," Harry added, "even if you do manage to take down a deer, this time of the winter they'll be skinny and plenty tough to chew. No roasting them over an open fire, only stewing the meat will make it worth eating."

"Yeah, I know, but the men need meat. I'm beginning to have my doubts that Boss Man Woods will have left a decent enough credit for what we need."

"You're not the only one with doubts. I'm just hoping Axel will be able to get feed for the horses. They need more than dried hay to keep doing the hard hauling work they do." Tarmo frowned and shook his head. "Fine mess we're all in."

It was past the middle of February before Axel returned. Ellie heard the scraping of the wagon's skids sliding over the crusty snow before she saw him. Her heart sank when she saw Axel. He looked like he'd aged ten years since he left. And the wagon was half empty. Ahni ran outside to see, too. Her heart jolted. Jalmer was not with Axel.

Axel reined the horse to a stop and jumped down. "Don't even bother welcoming me back," he said. "When you hear what I have to say, you'll wish you hadn't. Where is everyone?"

"Tarmo's out hunting. Harry and Flora brought bean soup out to the logging site for lunches—such as they are. They should be back soon. I hope Tarmo isn't out too late trying to follow a deer trail."

"Well, most of what I have here is grain for the horses. For us humans, I have a big sack of ham hocks. A smaller one of candles. Harry knows how to make candle soup, doesn't he? Well, he might have to learn. I hope our flour, corn, beans, peas, potatoes and such are going to hold for the rest of the season."

"Ooof! That is bad news. Thank goodness we at least have some of those."

"Port Charles is hurting for food stuffs, too. Even if Mr. Woods had left more credit, there wasn't much to buy. Most of the store shelves are empty. Folks who have never hunted or fished are learning fast. Everyone is praying for an early thaw so the road will open up. Then horses and wagons can bring supplies."

When Harry, Flora, and Ahni returned to the cook shack, they immediately got busy making bread, peeling potatoes, and adding them to the left-over bean soup from lunch. Ahni noticed Axel pull Harry aside for a moment and slip him a small leaf-wrapped packet. She hoped it was something special for her. As she scrubbed, peeled, chopped, and stirred, she thought of all the good things that could be in the packet. It was much too small for hard candies or a square of fudge. It was big enough for a tiny bit of sugar. Dreaming about something sweet melting in her mouth, she realized how tired she'd gotten standing and running back and forth getting whatever Harry called for. She saw Mam leaning against the back wall. Mam ran her hands over her tummy that was now protruding quite a bit. Ahni had been taking over more and more of her mother's work, but now, she needed to rest, too. She sat down on a sack of potatoes and watched her mother.

Ahni had just taken a boot off to rub her foot when Harry called to her, "No time for sitting and day dreaming. Bring a few of those onions. And chop them up for the soup."

Ahni frowned. She wished the holey ghost hadn't put a baby in Mam's belly. She wished she didn't have to do so much of her work. Ellie had told her not to complain. If she and Mam wanted to stay there, they'd have to work. And if Mam couldn't do it, Ahni had to do more. Ellie was helpful, too. She did most of the heavier work, but Ahni noticed that Tarmo no longer helped in the cook shack because he was spending more time hunting. He hadn't even swung Ahni around in circles for a long time.

"Look these onions. All soft and squishy." Ahni brought several to show Harry.

"Looks like they froze. We can still use them in soup. Sort them out. We'll use the softest ones first."

Just then Tarmo came in stomping snow off his boots and shaking the chills off himself. "No luck! I followed a trail for what seemed miles. At least tomorrow I'll know where to start."

Harry and Ellie both groaned. Ahni knew what the groans meant. She hoped she wouldn't be blamed for Tarmo not getting a deer.

"Now that you're all here," Axel started, "I'll tell what else I learned on my trip. Boss Woods's agent told me that Woods has heard tell of acres and acres of white pines further up north. He'll send Reino to look it over. He wants a huge camp set up there for next winter. He wants it big enough for a hundred or so loggers. One of my jobs will be to hire on a lot of men. That won't be too hard because lots of Swedes and Finns coming in from the old country are looking for jobs and land. Many logged in the old country so are good workers. And Indians who want to do something other than hunting and fishing in the winter. Plenty of good workers like Cloudy, White Wolf, and Big John we have here." Axel stopped to stir the tin mug of cedar tea Harry set before him.

"Bigger camp? What for?" asked Tarmo.

"He finally figured out that if he goes bigger into lumbering, he can afford to buy more land for railroads faster. He wants us to break our backs making him rich so he can get richer."

Tarmo added, "He's smart all right. He's figured out that after we cut down all the good white pine, and the profit in logging dries up, he'll still have his railroads."

"Cutting all the forests—he doesn't think that will ever be possible. There's another problem that our friends Cloudy and Big John have talked about. As it is, some of the tribes are already upset because when a logging camp comes near one of their villages, the trees are cut. The animals leave. Logs clog the rivers during spawning season. That means fewer fish. Logs also jam up in calm inlets and damage *manoomin* beds that the Indians depend on for food during the winter. In other words, their food supply is threatened every which way because of logging."

Ellie asked, "So, Woods wants a bigger camp. He wants to take down more trees and ruin waterways. The result will take good hunting grounds from the Ojibwe, possibly starving them in the winter, and he won't pay us until the camp closes in the spring. What other good news do you have?" Ellie nudged Flora and the two started chopping withered apples.

"Well," Axel wiped his nose on a red handkerchief, "Rumors are that this whole area will become part of the new Minnesota Territory by next year. And everyone is hoping it will become a state soon after that. Most of the lands east of us have already become states."

"And how will that affect us?"

"More settlers will come. They'll need logs and lumber to build houses and towns. Some will get rich. Others—like us—will break their backs getting them rich."

Ahni had been listening to the adults as they talked about too much logging and Indians going hungry because of it all. Some of what they said seemed as murky as mud to her. Hunger she understood. She didn't want White Wolf and his friends to go hungry because there weren't any fish, and that the deer left to find other forests to live in. As she listened, her mind wandered. It wandered to the little leaf packet Axel had slipped to Harry without saying a word. She'd hoped it was a good surprise for her, but now she knew. She knew just like she knew an axe would chop Jalmer's leg and that there was a baby in Mam's tummy. Worst of all, she knew that the packet was not a sweet for her, but something bad. Something really bad.

CHAPTER 24

The sun strengthened as it rose earlier and set later during the last days of February. Ahni squinted in the bright sun whenever she was outside. If any snow fell, it was beautiful big flakes that floated gently through the air. Ahni spun in a circle as she caught flakes on her tongue when she had to scoop buckets of snow to bring inside to melt for dish water.

With the sun came warmer weather and the thaw. The trails iced during the cold nights and became soft and slushy during the day. In the dim morning light, Ahni watched the loggers walk on top of the snow on their way to breakfast. By the time they left to go to the woods, the night cold that had crusted the snow had warmed. The men had stay on the slick path or else sink to their knees in soft snow.

Little by little Axel's story of his trip to Port Charles filtered through the camp. There hadn't been a doctor. Anyone who knew even a little about medicine couldn't do anything for Jalmer's leg except one Finnish woman who cleaned the wound. She knew about the plants that stopped bleeding. She said Jalmer was lucky the poultice had been used, otherwise, he would have bled to death. She had shaken her head as she felt Jalmer's forehead and pronounced him feverish with an infection.

"I met with Boss Woods's man and heard all the bad news. The only good news was that each of you can collect your season's pay any time in May. The bad news is that you have to go to Port Charles to get it. Unfortunately, the promissory note you'll get is only good at the dry goods store there. You'll find Woods's man, there. I'll be there, too, making sure you all get paid. I think Boss

Woods wants you all to come so he can sign you up for next year's big logging camp. And you've heard the other bad news already. No supplies except for the horses. For us, it's candles and fatty pork hocks."

It was a Sunday when Axel delivered all that last news. Needless to say, there was an uproar. "What? We can only buy goods we need at one place? At Port Charles? It's the opposite direction from where I live. Going there will use up days I could use in the fields or fixing the roof on our house or a million other things."

After the groanings were over, Ellie asked, "What about Jalmer?"

"When I couldn't find help for Jalmer in Port Charles, I brought him to Old Biddy Bones."

Harry looked at Flora while Axel stopped to sneeze and wipe his nose. She looked down at her swollen belly.

"She said to leave Jalmer so she could get his fever down. Cure his infection. Sew up his leg. She wanted me to stay and take down a deer to pay her for his care, but I had to get back."

While Ahni washed dishes, she tried to remember everything that had been said about Old Biddy Bones. Some said she could cure just about anything. A few loggers had said she was just a made-up story—like *Wiindigoo*. Now Ahni knew Old Biddy Bones was real.

Flora worked beside Ahni swishing dishes in the hot rinse water and setting them in the drying rack. Harry stood beside Flora reaching for the sour dough starter on the shelf above. In a flash—just a flash—Ahni saw the little leafy packet in Harry's hand as he showed it to Flora and gave her a smile. It was real. It wasn't like seeing the axe fly and chop Jalmer's leg. In another flash, Harry set the little packet back on the high shelf next to where he kept the bowl of starter. Ahni's heart thumped. Her palms sweat. It was just a little packet. Why did she have the feeling it was something bad?

That night, Ahni couldn't sleep thinking about the leaf-covered packet. She tossed and turned. She itched and scratched and hoped her bed wasn't full of fleas. When she did sleep, she dreamed a horrible dream. Big Thunder kicked his way out of a muddy grave. He rose like a mighty horse—a horse like Pegasus in the story—mud and slime dripped from his body. He snorted once, then stumbled. In her dream, Ahni ran to help him up. He struggled to stand. She tried her hardest, but he slid back into the ooze. At the last moment before his head sank completely below the surface, he quaked and hacked a gravelly cough. Out flew a baby horse covered with slime and goo. Ahni picked up the baby horse and cradled it gently.

The dream was so real that when Ahni shook off her sleep, she thought she could still feel the slick wetness of the colt. She could even smell the muddy quagmire Big Thunder had risen from. She wanted to sleep some more, to hold the colt in her arms, to wipe the gooey stuff off him, to see how beautiful he was. And she wanted him to not be just a dream, but for real. She'd take care of him, raise him to be strong and fast. He'd be her horse. They'd ride through the forest together. They'd swim in the lakes and rivers. Ahni would even sleep in his stable with him. They'd always be together. In the dim light of early morning, she mourned that he was just a dream. She so wanted him to be real.

The next Sunday, Ahni sat by Cloudy and White Wolf listening to them discuss the huge logging camp Mr. Woods planned for the next season. "No good can come from it. A hundred men? What are they trying to do? Cut down all the forests?"

The two of them nodded in agreement. "I'm not signing up for any more logging. For what? For a white man's piece of paper that we can only use at their stores? I'd rather trade furs and fish and baskets for what I need. I'll live the way our people have always lived—off the land, the rivers, and the lakes. Brother deer will feed me and my family. The fresh blue waters will quench our thirst. The fish of the rivers will jump into our nets. My family will join together and harvest enough *manoomin* for the whole winter. I will give thanks to the Creator the whole time."

"My favorite season is when the Harvest Moon shines and the *manoomin* is ready for picking," said White Wolf. "We line a shallow pit with the skin of our brother, the deer. All of us, even the little ones, put on moccasins we only use for the *manoomin* dance. We dance on the rice breaking the chaff away from the good. You should see the little ones dance. That's what makes it so much fun." He stopped while remembering how the little ones learned the dances from their grandmas and grandpas and then, in turn, teach the *manoomin* dances to their own grandchildren.

"Ya," Cloudy said, "My mother and all the mothers gently tap their drums while we dance. When we're done dancing, we put the *manoomin* in a shallow basket and call upon our friend the wind to blow away all that is not good to eat."

For a while, Cloudy tapped his knees like they were drums, then added, "I like when the whole family works together. We roast the *manoomin* over an open fire.

We work together taking turns stirring so it doesn't burn. Best of all, the whole time we tell our people's stories in the light of flickering flames."

"My favorite time," White Wolf chewed on a sprig of cedar while he said, "is when we tap the maple trees every spring. Young ones sit side by side with grandpas to whittle the taps. Together we watch and stir while boiling the sap into syrup. When I was little, I used to drink it before it was boiled. I liked it that much."

Cloudy put his arm around the younger man. "Changes are coming with the many new settlers. Already they're talking about railroads in the East. Big towns. Lots of people coming in the ships from across the wide waters will take the railroad following the setting sun. How long do you think before they discover our beautiful lands up here in the north and take them for their own?"

White Wolf answered, "Boss Man Woods already has. More and more settlers come and claim that what has forever been ours, is now theirs. They show pieces of paper demanding we move because they now own the land. Or at least, that's what they tell us the paper means."

"I hope you're not right, but I'm afraid you are. We've already seen the greed of people like Boss Woods who cut more forests than they could possibly need. Build more railroads. Bring more people. Gone will be the deer, the fish, and the *manoomin.*" Cloudy's eyes teared as he spoke.

Big John, Matti, and Kalle came to sit in the circle. Big John shrugged sadly as he listened to Cloudy and White Wolf. "Maybe we, the Anishinaabe, will be gone, too. Gone with the trees and the deer. There'll be no place for us. Worse yet, they bring new diseases that our medicine can't cure. The life our grandparents knew—it is gone."

Matti joined in. "Ya, this happened in the old country, too. My ancestors lived in harmony with the reindeer. Their seasons were our seasons. We followed them from grazing grounds to grazing grounds. My *mummo* told me the stories of our long-ago people. Then the strangers came." Matti wiped his eyes remembering. "They came and threatened to scatter and kill the herds of reindeer if our people didn't convert to their beliefs. Some converted to save the herds that fed us, clothed us, provided shelter, and even transportation. My *mummo's* father was one of the stubborn ones. He wouldn't give up his ancestors' way of life and beliefs. They burned him at the stake. They forced my *mummo* to watch." Matti's voice was almost a whisper as he spoke.

Cloudy put his hand on Matti's shoulder. "I didn't know your people had suffered like ours. We are brothers in our pain and memories."

Matti said, "Ya, I thought I had left all that behind when I packed my bundle and boarded the ship. My *mummo* told me to tell I was from Finland. That I was Finnish. She didn't want me to be made fun of and called a savage like I would have been if I said I was of the reindeer people."

Kalle sat next to Matti. "You and I are alike in that way. I gave up who I was, and who my people were to come here, too, only to find the Anishinabeg are treated the same way."

CHAPTER 25

After their big discussion, Cloudy, White Wolf, Matti, and Kalle chopped a hole in the river ice and fished until well after the sunset. When they had a nice catch to fry, they scaled each fish. Then they slit each one from the vent hole to its mouth. Ahni liked helping so when the fish were cut wide open, she slid her finger along the spine and pulled the insides out. White Wolf and Kalle separated everything and told her the names of what had been inside the fish. Then they made a game of it.

"Swim bladders!" Kalle said, "Find the swim bladders." Ahni searched for all the whitish air-filled sacs and put them in a pile.

Matti called out, "Stomach and guts." Everyone laughed.

Then Harry came over and said, "What Matti calls *guts* are really the intestines."

Ahni found the slimy, wiggly blobs easily.

Cloudy took a turn asking for livers. By now Flora and Ellie came to watch as Ahni piled them next to the swim bladders.

Kalle said, "Heart and kidneys."

"That easy!" Ahni said. "I find fast cuz not much else left 'cept more yucky stuff." "No bean soup for supper!" Harry started heating his big cast iron griddle.

To Ahni, it had been the best Sunday they'd had for a long time. She didn't even mind that there hadn't been enough loggers willing to hold the edges of a blanket to toss her into the air. The men who sat at the other table, not the one Cloudy, Kalle, and her other favorite men sat at, didn't talk to her at all. They gave her funny looks and would never come close to her. If she accidentally brushed one's shoulder when she brought platters of bread to their table, they'd brush off the spot like it was dirty.

Despite all that, she learned another song on Axel's accordion and played it until she could find all the keys without looking. When it was pitch dark, she ran to use the slop bucket in the stable before going to bed. On her way back she looked to the sky hoping to see Pegasus flying high above her in the stars.

When she returned, Espen closed his black book and told those who'd stay to listen, "Enough for tonight. Remember to cleanse yourself and your bunk of all evil before settling down for the night." Sven turned to Ahni and sneered.

Flora shivered a bit when she saw how Sven and some of the others treated her daughter. She herself didn't know what to make of Pap claiming Ahni was born bad because she was born during an eclipse. He'd said she caused Big Thunder to die. She didn't think it was possible that anyone, much less a sweet little girl could be born bad or cause a horse to die. But then there were other things she didn't understand. How had Ahni known that there was a baby growing in her belly when she had just begun to be aware of it herself? And what about her seeing the strange looking man in the tree when no one else had seen him? And she knew when Jalmer was cut by an axe. She even heard some muttering about Ahni being responsible for Alfred going missing.

She wished she could talk. Flora searched in the wood box where Ellie had thrown a page from her calendar. On the back she wrote *Do not tell anyone ever again you were born during an eclipse.* Some people were superstitious and would believe anything, or use any excuse to explain something that seemed unexplainable. She hoped her daughter would understand it was dangerous.

When Ahni came back in, she said to Mam and Ellie, "When outside, no see man in trees, and no find Pegasus in stars."

Shaking his head, Harry looked at the girl and then at Flora. *If only the girl didn't make matters worse by saying such strange things that no one else knew what she was talking about.* Flora shook her head, too, and handed Ahni the page where she'd written her warning.

Ellie had torn the February page off her calendar a few days earlier. The first week of March arrived warm and sunny. The snow melted during the day, yet the nights were cold enough so a crust formed that could be walked on until the sun reached full strength.

"Nice out. Don't need big sweater. Maybe summer come." Ahni found Tarmo in the stables scooping up and throwing out manure that had collected during the night.

He leaned against his shovel and said, "Don't be too eager for summer. If the thaw comes this early, the camp will have to close. Besides, the old folks say that if March comes in like a lamb, it'll go out like a lion."

"Not this year. March be all lamb."

Tarmo hung his shovel on nail. He wondered if Ahni was saying something else that would come true. Puzzled, he changed the subject. "What'll you do when the camp closes for the summer, and you can't come and pester me whenever you want?

"I no pester you. I help if you let me."

"Can't let you go back to cooking our food after playing in horse pucky. Harry wouldn't like that."

"Don't care. I like you better 'an I like Harry. He no like me none."

"Oh, he likes you plenty good. Says you're a good worker and never complain."

"He never tell me that. Just say 'Go get snow to melt. Peel potatoes. Wipe tables. Wash dishes.' I know what to do. He no need boss me alla time. He like Mam better."

Tarmo knew there was truth to that. Ellie had told him what she'd heard and seen many times. It worried both of them. He wanted to change the subject again so he said, "Let's go see if we can get a mug of hot tea and if Harry doesn't have a job for you, we'll play some Cats in the Cradle and get our fingers all tangled in the string."

Reino, the logging boss, fretted as the days warmed. The horses sweat under their heavy loads and had to be wiped off frequently so they wouldn't chill as they stood waiting for the sledge to be loaded again. That took time away from other jobs that needed to be done.

Worse yet, was that the snow was softening so fast it became slush beneath the horses' large hooves. Wet all the time, the hooves could get soft and crack and chip. Fungal infections could set in. If that happened, there'd be big trouble. He and Tarmo spent hours drying hooves and checking them for problems after the teams came in for the night. Tarmo even started going out to the logging site to care for the horses. That took time away from tracking deer. There was no more venison to add to the bean soup. The loggers suffered quietly in the mess hall, but let off their steam in the bunkhouse as they hung their sweaty socks and shirts to dry.

"That girl is nothing but bad luck."

"The thaw is happening too early and too fast."

"That's what happens when you bring a young girl into camp. She doesn't belong here."

"A girl born during an eclipse at that!"

"No ham. No tobacco. That's what she's brought upon us. Bad luck!"

Big John stepped in. "That can't be her fault. Be reasonable. She works hard. She's doing the work of two, now that Flora is big with child."

"That's another thing," Espen said, "We're low on food, but Flora still eats even though she doesn't do much work. The girl was born when the sun was blotted out in the middle of the day. That's a bad sign. I say she brings bad luck to the camp. Alfred's missing. We're starving. Jalmer got cut bad. First, we couldn't work because of a freezing spell. Now we're having an early thaw. None of that's normal. That girl is the cause. She's bad through and through."

As Espen talked, he glared at Big John and the others who stood with him. "She may look sweet as can be. She maybe even works hard. But underneath it all, she is an evil being. Hiding and waiting for a chance to do away with all of us. Just wait and see. You won't escape either."

Big John snapped back. "Quit blaming her! There is no such thing as being born bad because of an eclipse!"

At that, bedlam broke out. The men forgot about hanging their wet clothes. They tossed soggy socks at each other. Wet shirts hurled across the room. Cuss words flew back and forth in at least three, if not four, different languages. The spit and venom with which curses were shouted gave no doubt as to what they meant. The men pushed and shoved. They tore each other's bunks apart. They tangled and struggled with each other. Sven kicked a saw. It flew across the room. A candle fell. After White Wolf shook Sven off his back, he scrambled to set it back in place before a fire started. Axel and Tarmo came in to see what all the yelling and cursing was about.

"Stop now! Burn this place down, and you'll sleep in snowbanks tonight. I won't even let you sleep with the horses!" Tarmo's warning stopped everyone in the midst of their next swing, push, or cuss words. He and Axel stayed in the bunk house until the men finished sorting out and rehanging their wet clothes and settling into their bunks muttering.

Axel collected all the candles. As he snuffed the last one, he said, "No more candles until I'm sure there will be no more of your rough stuff. This thaw is causing enough trouble. I don't need you fighting each other. I don't care who started it and why."

CHAPTER 26

What else could go wrong? That was the question Axel, Tarmo, and Reino struggled with well into the night. Over-riding all their concerns about the short supply of food stuffs and the loggers at each other's throats, was the early thaw.

The thaw. Most Northwoods people were probably rejoicing. To them it meant planting their gardens early. A longer growing season. Warmer weather meant using less wood to heat their cabins. That meant less time in the woods restocking for the next winter. It also meant taking off long woolen underwear and hanging it to air out after a long winter.

Conditions in the woods grew worse. Clumps of snow from high branches fell on the men as they chopped below. The horses sank into deep slush as they pulled the sledges full of logs to the river bank. The ice was breaking up on the river. Soon the swift currents would carry the logs downstream to Mr. Woods's sawmill. Reino helped sharpen saws as he worried about the safety of the loggers and the horses. If a falling tree didn't kill a man, he could get whirled away from the river's edge when dams of ice broke. If he didn't drown under an eddy of freezing water, he could be pulverized by the pounding of the logs as they whooshed and roared around boulders and down waterfalls.

Tarmo worried, too, as he checked the horses' hooves. He looked for fungal growth and infections, but also worried about the lack of enough feed to keep them healthy as they pulled tremendous loads. Besides that, they could get caught too near the river banks when the ice cracked and rose like high ice walls sweeping everything in their path down the river.

In the cook shack, Harry worried about the supplies and the complete lack of any meat except for the fatty bits that clung to the pork hocks. Maybe the early thaw was good. Maybe he'd have at least one hock for each soup pot. Maybe the cold would come again, extending the season, and he'd run out of hocks. He worried as he kicked snow off the wanigan he'd made a short six or seven months ago to be ready for the log drive in the spring. That spring was just about here. He knew what he had to do. When nobody was looking, he checked to make sure the packet was still on the shelf where he kept it hidden. He'd have to use it soon.

Meanwhile, Axel worried about everything from the lack of supplies, the men fighting, the thaw, the coming log drive, Flora's pregnancy, Ahni's rather unique ability to predict what might happen which scared some of the loggers. He'd be happy if the thaw came faster so the girl and her mother would be on their way back home, and he'd never hire them on again.

Flora worried, too. Her belly swelled making it difficult to help in the cook shack. Harry wanted her to go with him on the wanigan during the log drive. He begged her not to go back to her lazy husband. He was so kind and thoughtful that she wanted to go with him, but he didn't want Ahni, especially not on the log drive. He said the wanigan was too small for more than the men who'd drive the logs, himself, and Flora. He said that none of the men would want Ahni on the drive either because she'd be bad luck. Flora missed her mother. She wondered if Tarmo and Ellie would care for Ahni and help her get back to Grammy. Her biggest worry was about her baby. What would she do if it was born during the log drive? She'd heard the drives were dangerous. Harry had told her not to worry. He had something to take care of the baby, but he hadn't explained what or how.

Ahni wanted one thing. That was for Mam to go home with her to Grammy. She hoped Pap had gotten a new horse so he could work in the woods. Most of all, she wanted to be held—almost smothered—by Grammy's warm bosom. She wished so hard she could almost feel Grammy's arms around her and hear her voice whispering, "My sweet, dear Lamb-i-kins." She wanted the snow to melt faster. She wanted Harry to climb onto the wanigan and pole it out into the middle of the river where the currents would sweep it away, out of Ahni's sight. Out of Mam's reach. As nice as Harry was to her when others were watching, she noticed a sharpness in his eyes when they carried buckets of snow in together, or when he reached for the bowl of sour dough starter and handed it to her. It was a sharpness that Ahni didn't like. She knew he'd put the little leafy packet on the high shelf, and she wanted it. She wanted to take it when he wasn't looking. She'd throw it way off onto the ice that softened and turned dark. Then she wouldn't have to worry about the packet anymore. Something told her that no good would come from it, but she didn't know what that was.

Ahni crossed her arms and set her jaw in a grim line. She knew what she had to do, and she had to do it soon.

CHAPTER 27

Harry no longer allowed Ahni to serve the men. He kept her out of sight in the cook shack. He, along with Tarmo and Ellie brought the giant kettle of soup to the loggers in the woods for their noon meal. In the evening, Flora and Ellie served the tables while Ahni mixed the heavy batches of dough for the next day's bread.

One day, when Harry was filling buckets with snow for melt-water, Ahni dragged a sack of potatoes below the shelf where the sour dough starter bowl was. She stood on the potatoes hoping to reach the little packet. Unfortunately, the potato bag wasn't full enough for her to reach that high. Hurrying before Harry came back in, she looked for something else to stand on. The benches the men sat on to eat were too heavy for her. There was a wood pile near the door. She grabbed one of the logs and stood on it. It rolled, almost tipping her to the floor. That wouldn't work.

Just then Harry came in lugging big pails heaped with snow. "What in tarnation are you up to now?" Ahni wobbled on the log. The sack of potatoes was still in front of the cook stove. "Clean up this mess and get busy doing something useful." His eyes were steely hard. Ahni shivered.

"Just getting' bowl down an' start makin' bread," she lied.

"Never do that yourself. You're not tall enough. You'll drop the bowl for sure. Spill the starter all over. Ruin it. Then the men will have something to complain about with flat bread and flapjacks tough as an old goat's hide. Bad luck girl. I'm beginning to believe it." Harry spit out his words and pounded the table.

That evening, the men finished eating and were pulling their hats over their ears to leave for the bunk house. As Sven walked by, he snarled at Ahni, "Big trouble in small package. Worst kind."

Flora heard, pulled her daughter away, and pointed for her start clearing the tables. Ellie told Ahni, "Finish cleaning up in here and do the dishes. Your mam and I will make the bread."

Ahni's legs shook as she cleared and wiped the tables. Then she swept the floor and pushed the benches back into place. They grated and groaned as she scraped them across the floor. Harry held his ears and said, "Pick the benches up instead of grinding them on the floor. It's annoying."

Ahni gave the last bench a shove despite what Harry had said. She'd never picked up the benches, and he'd never complained before. As she cleaned the mess hall, she looked up from time to time, Harry would be looking at her as if he was waiting for a moment to scold her again. She straightened her shoulders and set her jaw. She would not give him another chance to do that. The whole time she washed dishes, she thought hard about what she could stand on to reach the shelf where Harry kept the packet.

Ahni's chance came the next day. Harry, Ellie, and Tarmo left to deliver soup to the loggers in the middle of the day. Ahni was alone except for Mam who was lying down. Ahni heard her breathing deeply as she did when she slept. Ahni tip-toed to the store room. There she found the perfect thing. Light enough for her to carry. Tall enough for her to climb on and reach the shelf above the cook stove. There were two wooden casks. One held oats. The other held what was left of the wrinkled apples. The oat barrel was still half full. She wouldn't use that. If it tipped, the oats would make a tremendous mess. She didn't want Harry to see her trying to scoop the oats back into the cask.

Ahni spun the apple barrel to the front of the cook stove. Her pride in finding something to stand on didn't last long. The barrel had no cover, and it was higher than she could get on without something to step on first. As quietly as possible, so as not to wake Mam, she turned the barrel on its side and tipped out all the apples. Then she turned it upside down. Now all she had to do was get on top of it. Finally, she took a large cooking pot, turned it over, stood on it and was able to make her way up. The barrel was steady and stable. Ahni was not. The effort made her legs quiver and shake. Plus, she was fearful. Fearful of the height. Fearful Mam would waken. Fearful Harry would catch her.

Her fears became reality when Mam patted her on her leg just as she reached to feel for the packet. Ahni almost fell off the barrel. Mam frowned at her and signaled for her to come down. W-H-Y-? She wrote on Ahni's hand.

"Want packet."

W-H-Y again.

"It bad. Need find it. Need hide it. Toss it away on rottin' ice."

Mam stooped to help Ahni put the apples back in the barrel. Each time Ahni said something about the packet, Mam shook her head and frowned.

Finally, Ahni asked, "Do you know what in the packet an' why Harry keep it secret?"

After her mam nodded her head, Ahni said, "Tell me so I no get in trouble findin' it."

Mam shook her head and pressed her finger to her lips. "Why it secret?" Ahni asked.

Mam drew her daughter into a hug, but Ahni struggled away. If Mam wouldn't tell her, she would keep trying to get it and destroy it. She knew with certainty that what was in it was no good. She knew that with the same certainty she knew day followed night, and that after snow thawed, warm weather came.

The next few days were unhappy ones for Ahni. No one had time to play Cat's Cradle or give her words to spell or numbers to add. On Sunday, Axel didn't even bring out his accordion to teach her a new song. "Too busy." Everyone in the cook shack was too busy, and the loggers were too tired after their days in the woods. The wet, heavy snow made everything slower and harder. Ahni noticed the men were more sluggish.

"No meat," Big John explained to her. "We eat and fill our bellies with beans, but they don't stick with us. We have to work hard, but our muscles get tired. Our legs wobble. We get tired slogging through the wet sloppy snow. The horses, too, have trouble struggling through the slushy snow pulling sledge loads of logs. We could put fewer logs on each load, but then they'd have to make more trips. Which would be better? We don't know."

"The best thing right now would be to call it a season," said Matti. "I'm tired of all this and am even more sure than ever that I'll join a wagon train to California. No more logging and harsh winters for me."

White Wolf and Cloudy looked at each other. "Exactly what we've been thinking. Not the California part, but being done with this season. Not enough food. Too fast of a thaw makes everything more dangerous."

"I can't wait to get back to my family and to see how my young ones have grown."

"Maybe we should just leave now even if Axel won't call the season done. Roads will be mushy and muddy—impassable within a week if this keeps up. Rivers will open, and it'll be impossible to cross them to get to our village if we don't go soon."

Ahni chewed her nails as she listened. Her friends were already planning what they'd do when the camp closed. She was eager to get back to Grammy. As she worried, an image flashed before her eyes. In that instant she knew that Mam would float down the river on the wanigan with Harry. The image showed Mam and Harry, but Mam was not holding a baby. And Ahni was not with them on the wanigan. A shiver ran up Ahni's spine. Now she knew. Mam would go with Harry leaving her and the baby behind. Pap would yell and explode when he found out. The shiver came again. It was not good. She had to convince Mam not to go.

CHAPTER 28

Harry unwrapped the leafy packet and shook bits of root, fragments of dried leaves, and crushed seeds into a steaming cup of water.

"Your tea, Flora," he said as he handed the mug to Mam.

"Me, too," Ahni reached out wanting to taste whatever had been in the packet.

"Not this tea," Harry said. "Put a spray of cedar on hot water. Let it steep for a while for your own drink."

"Want what Mam has." Ahni crossed her arms and glared at Harry wondering why he'd emptied the whole packet into her mother's tea and not left any for himself or anyone else."

Harry shoved Ahni aside. "If you don't want cedar tea, go to bed."

Ahni ran to Mam and hugged her while trying to push the mug and spill it all to the floor. Flora hugged her daughter, but held tightly onto the mug.

"No drink." Ahni whispered into her mother's ear, but Mam didn't listen and quickly drank from the mug.

"Go to bed, now!" Harry scowled as he roughly squeezed Ahni's arm. "I don't want trouble from you."

It was too late to throw the packet away or keep Mam from drinking the tea, so Ahni went to bed. Later, she awoke from her dream trembling. Big Thunder had risen from the muddy ooze again, but he had turned and run away from her. She'd called for him to stop, to let her climb onto his broad back so they could gallop away to find green pastures and warm themselves in glades of sunlight.

Chilled, she reached to snuggle into the ragged blanket she and Mam shared. No blanket. No Mam. Ahni shivered again. A deep shiver. A shiver that was from more than not having a blanket to cover herself. A shiver that burned into hot fear.

Mam was gone with the only blanket they shared. Maybe she'd wrapped herself in it and gone to the stables to use the slop bucket. Ahni waited. Mam didn't return, but Ahni's fear did, and it grew with each passing moment.

She sat upright. Her shoulders quaked. A sense of overwhelming dread overcame her. She took a deep breath, stood, and tried to shake off her fears. *What was there to be afraid of? Mam was probably just in the stables listening to Ellie and Tarmo talk about their day. She would be back soon.* Somehow, Ahni knew that wasn't so. She wasn't going to wait. While she tugged on her boots, she thought about Harry, the packet, and the mug of tea her Mam drank.

As soon as she left the cook shack, Ahni heard a strangled and unearthly moaning. It was so low she had to stop and listen to be sure she'd heard it. The eerie groan shook Ahni and intensified her fears. She ran toward it as fast as she could. Twice, she slipped on the icy path. Twice, she scrambled back to her feet ignoring the bloody scrapes on her palms. Twice, she yelled, "Mam, I'm coming!"

Inside the stables, Mam lay on a stack of straw. Her throaty rumblings shocked Ahni. She'd never heard her mother make any such sounds before. Ellie held a bundle as she knelt beside Mam murmuring comfort. "It is done. Your baby is born. Rest now."

Tarmo, Alex, and Harry stood off to one side holding lanterns; their faces grim and shadowed in the flickering lights.

Ahni ran to Mam. A musty odor mixed with that of the straw filled her nose. "Mam."

She reached for her mother's hand. Mam smiled weakly at her daughter. Mam's hand was clammy as she squeezed Ahni's.

Turning to Ellie, Ahni said, "Baby." She peered at the bundle wrapped with the only blanket that she and Mam had shared. A coating of slime and tissue covered the little baby's head and face.

"Boy," Ellie said as she wiped the baby's cheeks with a corner of her apron.

"Baby boy." Ahni reached for the baby. Just like in the dream she'd had of Big Thunder's colt, she wanted to wipe the gooey stuff off the baby. She wanted to see how beautiful he was. She held him in her arms wiping his forehead with her sleeve. He was real. Not like the colt in her dream. She put her thumb to his mouth. He gently suckled it for a moment, but only a moment. She vowed to herself to always take care of him, to raise him to be strong and fast. He was her brother. Together, they'd explore the forests. They'd swim in lakes and rivers. They'd pick berries and find mushrooms after the rain. Ahni would hold her brother while he slept. They'd always be together.

Even while Ahni gently rocked the baby boy, he never cried or cooed. Never made a sound. Never wiggled. Never suckled her thumb again. Tarmo came and held his lantern close. In the dim light, it was clear. The baby was blue. As Ahni brushed her fingers along his cheek, she felt the coolness of the baby. Too cool. She cuddled him closer, trying to warm him.

"Blue baby." Ellie wiped a tear away. She reached for the tiny bundle. Ahni pushed her away.

"What mean *blue baby*?" she asked as a tremor of dread coursed through her body again.

"It means the baby won't live. Maybe has already died." Ellie's voice was soft and halting.

"No! Baby no die like baby from Big Thunder! I no let him!" Ahni held her little brother closer and tighter. "I no let him die."

"Give the baby to your mother," Tarmo said gently, "Let her hold him one last time."

Ahni knelt by her mother. The same eerie moan slipped from between her lips as she put her arms out to hold the little boy. Ahni watched as Mam brushed her lips across his forehead and tears slid down her cheeks. "What we name him?" she asked.

Her mother just shook her head. Ellie put her fingers on the baby's wrist. Then she felt his chest and let her shoulders slump. Harry stepped forward. "He's gone. Time for you to let the boy go, Flora. Time to heal." He took the baby in one arm. The little boy's head drooped to one side.

Ahni yelled, "No!" She reached for the baby.

Harry turned his back and pushed Ahni away so she stumbled into a hay stack. "The baby is dead. It's late. We all need to get to sleep if we're going to work tomorrow. Life goes on!"

Ellie and Tarmo helped Ahni stand and brushed hay off her. "He's right," Ellie whispered. "The baby was born too soon. I'm so sorry, but there's nothing we can do for him. Right now, we need to get some sleep so we can do our jobs tomorrow."

"He did it!" Ahni screamed. "He kill baby. He make it born too early!" She lunged toward Harry.

Ellie and Tarmo held Ahni back. Nothing they said or did calmed the girl as Harry took the baby outside. "What he do with Mam's baby?" she cried.

"He'll put the baby somewhere. Maybe when the snow melts and the ground is soft, he can be buried." Tarmo patted Ahni on the shoulder as he spoke. Ahni didn't believe him.

"No! He need name. I give him Moses name. Like in story Espen read. They not kill Moses, but put him on little raft on river. Egypt princess find him and he live happy ever after and be good man. Not ever be man like Harry who give bad stuff to Mam to drink an' kill baby. We do what they do to Moses. Put him on little wanigan and float my little Moses down river. Someone good. Maybe princess find him. Take care of him."

A soft moan came from Flora who still lay in the hay with her eyes closed. Ellie knelt beside her and thought of the other stories Ahni had liked so much. The one about the Holy Ghost bringing a baby to Mary and Baby Jesus being born in a manger. Stories so much like what had happened, yet so different.

CHAPTER 29

That night, Tarmo and Reino carried wood into one of the domed steam huts so Flora could have a warm bath after giving birth. Ellie walked Ahni back to the cook shack.

"Sleep now. Your mam will come to be with you after her bath. Everything will be better in the morning. Let's hope for a nice sunny day."

"Want to know."

"Know what?" Ellie asked.

"Know how Mam cough up such big baby. I know belly grow when baby grow. But how big baby fit in Mam throat and mouth to be spit out?"

"Wherever did you get such an idea that babies are coughed up?"

"Dream about Big Thunder. He burp and cough up baby horse, but baby die. Die like baby Moses."

Ellie covered her smile with her hand. She finally said, "When you get older, you'll understand."

Ahni didn't like the answer. "Hummmff! That no answer!"

Tarmo came in to say that the steam bath was ready, so Ellie tucked Ahni into her bed and headed to help Flora. Tired as she was, Ahni couldn't sleep thinking about Mam's blue baby. Deep inside, her stomach roiled and sour bile filled her mouth as she thought of Harry emptying the whole packet into the mug to make tea for her mother. She couldn't shake the feeling that it was all Harry's fault that the baby was born too early. Born blue. She didn't like that big people kept secrets. Big people thought she was too young to know some things. But they were wrong.

She knew some things they didn't know. She was sure that Harry had killed her baby brother, and if they had wrapped him warmly and put him on a wanigan to float down the river, then she, Ahni, could find him someday.

After Flora had bathed and crawled into bed with her daughter, Ahni was still not comforted. She wanted to be held, but not by Mam. Mam had changed. She wasn't going home to Grammy with her. She was going on the wanigan with Harry. With a sob, she inched as far away from Mam as she could.

When Ahni awoke shivering in the night, she smelled smoke. She still smelled smoke in the early hours of the new day. She even smelled smoke when she heard Harry come into the cook shack to start breakfast.

She still smelled smoke when she headed to the stables to relieve herself. She saw smoke rising from one of the domed steam baths. That wasn't right. The fire that had been set for Mam's bath should have been out a long time ago. Ahni shivered in the chill morning air when she headed to the domed steam bath to find out why it still had a fire going. By the time she entered, there were only the remains of embers glowing, so she headed to the cook shack to start her morning chores. All the time she wondered if others had taken late baths and kept the fires going.

All morning, Ahni felt like there were big clumsy boots on her feet as she dragged around setting out tin plates and mugs on the tables. Dark bags puffed under Harry's eyes. Ellie and Tarmo yawned as they went about their chores. Ahni was glad when Mam got up and helped carry platters of flapjacks, but she, too, was more tired and slower than usual. The loggers were always quiet as they ate quickly before heading to the woods. That morning they were even quieter. No one coughed or sneezed. They didn't even stomp their boots as they entered.

After the loggers left, Mam lay down to rest. Ellie and Ahni cleaned the mess hall. While Ahni washed dishes, Ellie helped Harry pour beans into the big pot and set it to start cooking. Harry usually set the beans to soak the night before, but hadn't done it last night. *Too busy killing baby,* Ahni thought.

"Leave the dishes until after you get some potatoes and carrots chopped into the soup pot. And hurry." Harry ordered angrily, as though he knew what Ahni was thinking.

Ahni pulled her hands out of the sudsy water. "Soup be no good. Beans be hard for noon meal. All because you busy killing Mam's baby last night and not soak beans!" Ahni spit out the words she'd been thinking as she headed to get the potatoes.

Harry roared, "Enough of that dead baby stuff! It was born blue. Nobody is to blame for that. Just like you were born to be bad during an eclipse. I suppose you think I'm to blame for that, too. Besides, if you know so much, you could've put the beans to soak."

Things didn't get better between Harry and Ahni. She did her work, but didn't talk to anyone. Not even to Ellie and Tarmo. Harry ordered her around even though she knew her jobs. She huffed and puffed, but did them just the same. Ahni's only comfort came from White Wolf and Cloudy after the evening meal. They offered to play Cat's Cradle with her, but she was in no mood to play.

"How about we tell you good story. Good Ojibwe story our grandmothers and grandfathers told us."

"What kind of story?" Ahni asked.

"Do you want to hear a story about a gift the Creator gave our people?"

"I like story about presents."

"Come outside, and we'll tell."

White Wolf spread cedar branches on the ground for them to sit on in the dim twilight. Big John came, too. He began to sharpen his saw with a file as Cloudy started the story.

"Long ago, our people lived simply. All summer and autumn, we gathered berries, mushrooms, and fish to dry for the long winter. We gathered *manoomin*, too, and hung venison to cure. But the winter winds were biting and cruel. Ice monsters froze the lakes and rivers."

"Not only that," added White Wolf, "but snows fell heavily. Our trails were blocked forcing us to stay in our birch and skin wigwams for many days. The sun peeked between clouds for short times, but its rays were weak and did little to warm us. We barely survived each winter."

Cloudy took the story up again. "We feared *Wiindigoo* would come to clutch us by his frightful clawed hands. By the time icicles finally dripped, and the sun became kinder and stayed longer, many had become weak and frail—barely living. With the coming of the warmth, the bear came out of his den. Buds on trees grew bigger. We were glad we could leave our wigwams."

Ahni wanted to ask about wigwams, but she stayed silent, waiting for more story.

"That's when, long ago, Brother Crow came and in all his wisdom, he taught our people how to peck holes in the maple tree to capture the sap that runs freely each spring. That sap gives life after the long hard winter. Not only the weak and frail, but everyone needs it to awaken their bodies and get strength. To this day, we praise Brother Crow each spring when we see him come back because that's how we know it's time to gather the special sap of the maple tree."

Big John stopped sharpening his saw and said, "That's why we always share maple sap with Crow, and we always thank the Creator for giving us the gift of such a wonderful tree."

"That good story," Ahni said. "There still trees like that?"

"Have you never tasted the sweet sap of the maple tree?"

"No. Never."

"Well, this Sunday, we'll take you to where there is a grove of maples. Maybe the sap will be running and you'll get a taste, but you must remember to thank the Creator and Brother Crow."

CHAPTER 30

The promised Sunday of tasting maple sap never came for Ahni. Two days before the awaited day, some loggers led a team of horses and a sledge loaded with logs to the edge of the river. At the same moment, a loud cracking and booming of the melting ice frightened the horses. They reared and surged forward just as a shelf of ice buckled and tore loose, sweeping its way down stream. Thick sheets of ice heaved. The panicked horses twisted in their harnesses causing the load of logs to tilt and tumble into the churning river, taking the horses with them, battering them, and holding them under water.

One of the loggers ran to the cook shack yelling, "Help! The horses are drowning! Bring knives. Anything we can use to cut them free of their riggings!"

Harry, Flora, and Ellie gathered knives and ran to the river bank. Trying to remain calm, Reino and Tarmo had already freed one of the horses and were struggling to avoid the flying hooves as the other horse screamed, nickered, and snorted as it tried to free itself. Ahni trailed a distance behind Mam and Ellie hoping Harry wouldn't see her and order her back to the cook shack. But he did see her.

"Get her out of here!" he yelled to Flora.

Sven and other loggers noticed. "We've had enough of her and her bad luck!"

"Get her out of here. Out of the camp. Far away, or we'll all be killed! Drowned!"

Flora and Ellie took Ahni by her hands and tried to hurry her away. Ahni rebelled. "I not be bad to horses. Big Thunder and Pegasus were horses, too. I like horses."

Mam held onto her tighter. "Hush!" Ellie warned.

It took a while for the second horse to be untangled of the jumbled leather straps that hitched the two horses together. Unfortunately, both horses had been under the icy water and battered by logs and slabs of ice too long. When Tarmo tried to get one horse back onto its feet, it strangled on its own mucus while trying to snort and cough out water. No matter how hard Harry and Alex tried to get the other horse up on its feet and breathing, it died, too. Meanwhile, Reino and the loggers struggled to empty the sledge and to right it before the raging waters and massive chunks of ice swept it down river.

The weary loggers trudged their way into the mess hall for their noon meal. Not only were all the men as somber as they'd ever been, but the bean soup was almost inedible. The one ham hock Harry had thrown in had not seasoned it one bit. The few potatoes and carrots didn't even help make it into a good soup. Fortunately, there were fresh loaves of bread, and a scant bit of apple sauce made from a few withered apples to save the meal.

The loggers headed to the woods as fast as they could after eating. Sven whispered to Harry as he left. "She'd better be gone before we come back. Or . . ."

Ahni didn't hear what else Sven said. Her heart thumped in her chest as she started clearing the tables. She was almost in tears thinking about what might happen to her now that so many believed that she caused the death of two horses as well as the wounding of Jalmer's leg. Flora reached to hug Ahni, but she ducked out of her mother's arms.

Harry said, "Leave her. We need to get busy."

Ahni had just finished washing dishes when Big John, White Wolf, and Cloudy came back into the cook shack.

"What you Indians doing here? You're supposed to be at the logging site!" Harry stirred a huge amount of sour dough starter into the mixing bowl.

Big John spoke for the three. "We're leaving now. With one less horse team, fewer loggers are needed. When we leave, there'll be more food for those who stay. We aren't needed for the log drive, so we're going now."

"Well, I'll be. Never have any loggers left the camp before the wood bosses say the season is over. Does Reino know this?"

"We already told him and Axel. Reino didn't like it because there are trees already down that need to be cut into lengths and gotten to the river bank before too long. Axel said he couldn't stop us, and there was good reason to what we said about the food."

"Then what are you doing here? You can get going now. And take that eclipse-born girl with you for all I care. She needs to go, too."

Cloudy spoke up. "We've talked about that. She'd be welcome at our village, but if we're caught traveling with a white girl, someone'll shoot or hang us from the nearest tree just to save her from being kidnapped by what they call *savage injuns*. You know that's true. And we know you don't want her on the wanigan even though you're taking her mam with you."

Harry scowled at Cloudy. "Clear your stuff from the bunk house and get going!"

White Wolf took Ahni's hand and brought her to sit at one of the tables with him. "We'll miss you. And we'd take you if it weren't so dangerous for us. You need to go home to *Gookomis*—your Grammy." Tears came to Ahni's eyes.

Cloudy and Big John joined them at the table. "We each have a gift for you to remember us by." With that White Wolf gave Ahni a little grey stone. "Stone," he said, "but not just any stone. Stone that's small but strong. Hard to break. It'll endure many winters. Many seasons. It's already very old, and will last until you and I and our children and children's children have all passed from this earth. Keep the stone in this little pouch. Keep it with you. Hold it when you're afraid. Hold it when you're alone. Remember to be strong and unbreakable like it is."

Ahni held the stone in her hand. It fit perfectly into her palm when she clenched it tightly. She smiled at White Wolf and thanked him. "I no have gift for you," she said.

"Your smile is your gift. Thank you." He patted her shoulder.

Cloudy gave his gift next. "This Jackpine cone has fallen from its tree. It looks dead, but is not. It has life in it. Lots of life. The seeds of life are sealed tightly inside it. The woody scales protect the seeds inside until they open and release the seeds. Then the seeds grow into a whole new forest. That could happen many years from now. Be like the pine cone. Protect all that is inside you. Think of the seeds as who you can be—protected and hidden until the right time."

Ahni wasn't sure she understood all that Cloudy said, but she held the pine cone, fascinated by what lay hidden inside. That hard woody outer shell protected the insides. That's what she needed. A hard shell to protect herself for what was to come next. And to be unbreakable like the stone.

Last was Big John. He took her hand, opened her fingers and spread some seeds into her palm. *"Manoomin,"* he said. "Wild rice. The food that grows on water. A gift to the Anishinaabe Ojibwe from the Great Creator. It's the food we need through long cold winters, before the Crow comes in the spring. We give these grains to you, hoping you will never be hungry. Our people always give thanks while gathering the rice."

As Ahni fingered the small grains, Big John said, "Each grain gives life to a whole new plant and that plant makes more grains. Grains to eat. Grains to grow more plants." Ahni understood. Grammy always saved squash seeds for the next spring so they'd have more squash.

"I put the *manoomin* with the pine cone and stone into this little pouch made from the skin of Brother Deer." White Wolf handed the pouch to Ahni. "Carry it with you always. Each gift we've given you will give you everything you need."

"Remember to give thanks as you pick berries or take anything for yourself from the Creator's gifts." White Wolf tied the pouch around Ahni's neck.

Ahni promised, "I'll give thanks alla time. Even now. Thank you."

CHAPTER 31

Cloudy, White Wolf, and Big John left. Ahni felt special as she held the pouch. When she remembered each gift, she felt less alone. Then Harry ruined her thoughts when he called her to stir the bean soup.

"You have to leave before the men return from the woods." He said it softly, but his eyes were steely.

Ahni felt alone again. She touched the stone in the pouch. *Be strong like stone.* "Mam come with me?" She looked at her mother who seemed to shrink before her eyes.

"Flora is coming with me on the wanigan. I'll need her help cook for the men. You can't come. No room for you. And the log drivers would quit before going on the dangerous trip down the river with you anywhere in sight." His voice wasn't so soft anymore.

Ahni looked to Mam. Flora nodded her head, slid her hands over her shrunken belly, and then shifted her eyes to the floor. "After wanigan you come home? To Grammy? To Pap? To me?" Ahni's voice broke. She already knew the answer, but she wanted Mam to answer—to either shake her head, or to nod.

Harry answered for her. "Flora is going to stay with me."

Mam tore a page from Ellie's calendar and started to write on the back. Ahni's lower lip quivered as she read out loud what Mam had written. "I can't go back to Pap. He won't work. He won't bring food home. He left us here. You go back. Grammy will take care of you."

What she'd seen in a flash was true. Mam wanted to be with Harry. Ahni felt her heart become as hard as the little stone in her pouch. *Mam no longer my Mam.*

She Flora. Harry's Flora. Ahni's tears fell as she felt the pouch for the stone. *Be strong.* But Ahni couldn't be strong. Not yet, maybe when the pine cone opened, and its seeds fell to the forest floor, maybe then she could be strong, but not now.

Crying, she ran out of the cook shack. She ran to the stables, but the rich odors of the horses reminded her of the horses that had died at the river. She ran to the domed birch steam bath hut. The embers had all died. No fire warmed the inside, but she curled close to the fire pit anyway and sobbed until there were no more tears for her to cry. As she wiped her eyes clear, she noticed something at the far edge of the circle of ashes. Picking it up, she realized that it was a scrap of the ragged blanket she and Mam had shared through the whole winter until . . . She fought to keep the thought out of her head, but it wouldn't go away. The blanket had been wrapped around her brother, Baby Moses—who should have floated down the river to be found by a princess. The thought—the knowing of what Harry had done to the baby was too painful for her to even think about. She put the scrap of singed blanket into her pouch with the stone, the pine cone, and the *manoomin.* She would keep it forever to remember.

Ellie found her there in the steam hut, curled up and holding the pouch. "Come, you must be freezing."

"I go to stables, but not cook shack. Mam—I mean Flora—and Harry no want me." Ahni remembered how good Ellie and Tarmo had always been to her, and how they once had said that if Flora had to return home to have her baby, they would take care of Ahni at the camp. So, she asked, "You let me hide in stables? When camp close, I go with you and Tarmo?"

Ellie put her hands to her mouth. Her eyes opened wide. "That can't be," she said. "Harry wants you to leave now. Tarmo and I have to stay and work until the camp closes and then we're going south to St. Anthony. We'll stay there a year or so until we earn enough money. Then we'll take a steamboat down the Mississippi to where the wagon trains start out for California. We can't take you with us. I'm sorry, but you have a father and grandmother. You need to go to them."

"Nobody want me." Ahni wailed. "Not Pap. He bring me an' Mam here. Maybe no want me back. Mam smart not go home. Maybe even Grammy not want me no more."

"Go inside. Say goodbye to your mam. Come back. I'll give you a horse blanket so you won't freeze."

Ahni felt like she'd been scooped hollow. Gone was everything she'd liked about this camp—food at every meal, accordion music on Sundays, blanket tosses, stories told by the men, Cloudy, White Wolf, and Big John. She wished she'd never been born during an eclipse. She might as well be as bad as everyone thought she was, so she wiped her eyes and clomped into the cook shack.

Crossing her arms and holding herself tightly, Ahni said, "Flora, I go now. We no see each other no more." Ahni didn't know why she said that, but as soon as she did, she knew it to be true. She'd never see her mother again. Without looking at Harry, she made a secret wish that the river would swallow him and never burp him up to breathe air.

Flora put her arms around her daughter, held her, and sobbed. When Ahni struggled away, she reached for Ahni's hand, wanting to write something on her palm, but Ahni clenched her fists. "I go now. You be happy." Before she could slip out the door, Flora took a fresh loaf of bread and tucked it under her daughter's arm.

Ahni ran out the door and to the stables before her stream of tears could blur her vision. Ellie met her there. "I have to get back to the cook shack to help with the evening meal before Harry starts yelling. It's been a bad day for everyone. Right now, it's late. Too late for you to start for home. Stay hidden here for the night. Don't let any of the loggers see you. In the morning you can start out when there's plenty of light to find your way."

Ahni nodded and started to burrow into a heap of straw. Glad she didn't have to leave so close to sunset, it suited her just fine to spend the night hiding. Even the jabs and pokes from the straw did not discomfort her as much as the harsh words from Harry or her mother abandoning her, or the painful truth that Ellie and Tarmo didn't want her either, or that it was too dangerous for her Ojibwe friends to take her to their village. The thought that they could be shot or hanged just because someone didn't know she was happy to be with them disturbed her most of all.

In the morning, Kalle and Matti cautiously entered the stables. "Ahni," they whispered. "We know you're here. Ellie told us. We're bringing you something for your journey home."

Ahni wasn't sure she should crawl out of her straw cave, but Kalle and Matti were friends. They'd sat at the table with Cloudy and the others and never made fun of them for being Indian. She shook the straw from herself, brushed her hair out of her eyes and stood to see the men.

"Ah, there you are. Look what we have for you." Kalle held out two withered apples. It was the best of the food left in the camp. Then Matti lifted his hat and pulled out a whole carrot. "Good thing Harry was too busy being grumpy this morning so he didn't notice we were helping ourselves to some of his precious food."

Ahni's slender shoulders shook. They were kind. They brought what she needed to keep from starving as she headed back home. Kalle held out his arms. She ran into them, but just for a second. "You need go to woods so Reino not wonder where you be. Big trouble if they know you with me."

"We're going. Look, Asko and Pentti sent you something, too." Matti pulled out two more carrots—one from each sleeve. And then another from inside his jacket. "This one is from Reino."

Ahni laughed despite all her troubles. "You magic. Find carrots everywhere."

"*Hyvästi.* Travel safely. We don't believe you were born bad, so don't you believe it either." Kalle and Matti nodded to her and slid out the door.

Ahni touched her pouch. She held the stone. It was time to be strong. She bundled the bread Mam gave her with the apples and carrots. Ellie wasn't in the stables, but she'd promised a horse blanket, so Ahni crept to the side where the horse stalls and all their gear usually were. It was empty now. Ahni found a blanket, a big one that she could wrap around herself if she had to sleep under a tree at night. She thought back to the time Pap had led her and Mam to the camp. They'd spent a night in a farmer's barn. She'd look for it on her way back.

CHAPTER 32

The healer shook her head. She should not have let the man with the axe wound stay. His leg was bad. Pus oozed. He was feverish. The healer shook her head. She was getting old and didn't think she could heal the man, but she'd try. She laughed to herself. Even if she couldn't help him, he'd still be good for something.

The healer plucked leaves and roots that hung from branches crisscrossing the ceiling of her hut. A sharp pain pricked her fingers as she reached for a bunch of dried leaves. The healer jerked her hand away. The sharp prick warned her away from those leaves. It always happened that way. A soft tingling meant the leaves, roots, or berries she plucked were good for the potion she was making. A sharp pricking told her that they were not. After choosing all the leaves and roots, she needed, she shook dried berries into her hand. A soft tingling tickled her fingers. She nodded, but was still nervous. She had never tried to heal such a deep and infected wound before.

The potion did not take away the man's pain. Even with the thick salve she spread on the gash, the gaping wound did not close. The healer worried. Maybe her hands could no longer choose the right leaves and roots. Maybe, the healing gift was leaving her. Maybe the damage from the axe needed something else. She spread more salve on the yawning wound and chanted.

Axe of might. Shed your bite.
Axe of iron. Shed your fire.
Axe of iron, be soft as earth that does no harm.

Day turned into night and back into day as the healer droned on and on. Needing sleep, she murmured, "They should have brought the axe with the wounded man. Then I could sing the axe to do no harm. Too late. Too late."

Ahni trudged along river banks and looped her way through the forest. She stumbled over tree roots and pushed her way through prickly bushes. She crossed deer trails, stepped over bear droppings, and heard wolves howling in the distance.

By the time the sun was low in the sky, her feet were sore, her stomach growled for another chunk of bread or bite of apple. She looked around. Nothing was familiar. She'd passed no farms. Seen no people. She was lost! She wished she were back at the camp. She missed the sound of loggers sharpening their saws and the smells of bread baking in the oven. A pang of loneliness overcame her. She felt the pouch at her neck and remembered her friends who'd given her the stone, the pine cone, and the *manoomin*. She held the stone. *Be strong.*

A high hill loomed in front of her. A frozen and snow-covered creek was on her left. She knew she should turn to walk along the creek's shore even though it looked rocky and dangerous, but at the same time, she felt a tug to climb the hill. *Too tired to climb hill. Need look for place to sleep.* She turned toward the creek, but the urge to climb the hill was strong. Taking a deep breath, she struggled her way up through crusted snow. *Maybe find good tree to sleep under.*

She almost walked by it, but when she heard a bird tweeting, she looked. A crested bird perched on a half-tipped dented bucket next to a wall of stacked branches and moss-chinked logs. *A place to rest and maybe spend the night?* Ahni walked along the lopsided wall. The logs and branches were lashed to trees at either end to keep the wall upright. That wall met another wall as haphazard as the first. It, too, ended at a tree and was fastened to its trunk. Altogether there were seven crooked walls. Each wall leaned precariously. The whole of it would have fallen if not tethered to trees. There were no windows. Ahni was fascinated by the rickety and ramshackle building. As she neared the low doorway, she wondered who possibly lived there.

Ahni raised her hand, ready to knock; the door opened. "Took your time getting here, didn't you? We've been waiting."

Waiting for me. For what? The door opened wider. Hidden in the shadows, Ahni saw a hand beckoning her to enter.

"Old Biddy Bones?" Ahni asked as she saw a dim outline of the person attached to the hand. Ahni had no idea why those three words had left her mouth, but it had seemed as normal as anything else she could have said.

"Is that what they're calling me these days?" the wraith-like figure asked.

"Ifn you be healin' woman who live far in woods all alone."

After pulling Ahni in by the arm and closing the door, the person said in a raspy voice, "I guess I am that . . . Woman? Did you just call me a woman?"

Ahni stared at the shadowy figure up and down. Baggy bibbed overalls. Well-worn and patched on both knees. Hiding any bodily curves. Thick slab soled boots with heels worn so unevenly that the person's foot tipped inward. A dusty shirt with ragged cuffs. Set above it all was a wrinkled bony face. Hair the color of straw. No beard! No mustache!

"I heard stories call Old Biddy Bones a woman."

"Well, then I'm a woman! Today, but maybe not tomorrow. For now, no more of this nonsense. We have a job to do, and I'm glad you came to help."

Ahni was more than bewildered. "I not here to do job. I kinda got lost in woods. Tryin' to find home, but find here instead."

"You came because you were needed. You're not lost. You're just not where you want to be at this moment in time. Time? What is time? Something to play with. Something that gets in the way." Old Biddy Bones stopped to wipe her sleeve across her nose. "Nevertheless, it is time for us to do our job or that poor man over there will run out of time."

Baffled, Ahni looked around the hovel. The pile of stacked logs and branches was just one cluttered room. Bunches of herbs, leaves, and dried roots hung from branches that made up the ceiling. Spider webs filled every possible nook and cranny. A small fire burned in a circle of stones. A pile of furs heaped on what might be a hammock hanging from the ceiling. On a raised plank that Biddy Bones called a table, ragged blankets covered what looked to be a person. A soft moan came from beneath the blankets.

"Jalmer?" asked Ahni when she remembered that Axel had brought him to Old Biddy Bones when he couldn't find a doctor in Port Charles.

"If that's the name of someone an axe tried to get the better of, then that's

Jalmer. I never ask names. Names never tell anything about a person. How they smell tells more."

Ahni stood next to the man on the table. "Jalmer," she whispered.

The man peered out at her. Jalmer looked different. His usual clean and trimmed beard was now shaggy and greasy. In a weak and scratchy voice, he said, "Ahni, the eclipse-born girl. What're you doing here? Causing more trouble?"

Old Biddy Bones interrupted. "No hard feelings here. Nothing but healing." She turned to Ahni and said, "Poisons from his infection might have traveled. Pain rattles his brain. There's only one way to get him up and walking his way home. Giving me back my table so I can sit down to a decent meal. We have to do it now."

Ahni watched Old Biddy Bones grab a handful of leaves and roots and stir them into a tin mug of hot water. After it had steeped a few moments, she dripped the liquid into Jalmer's mouth. He squirmed, tightening his lips. He coughed and gagged. He swung his head one way or the other to avoid swallowing any more of the liquid.

"You can help here. Hold his head while I pry his lips open. No way can I saw his leg off unless he drinks this."

Saw his leg off? Ahni shivered to think of it, but she held Jalmer's head still while Old Biddy Bones slid a wooden spoon between his lips and fed him the liquid.

"Now we wait until he sleeps. Then we take his infected leg. It's the only way to get rid of the poison. He got here too late. No other way. At least he'll still be able to walk with crutches. But no more logging for him."

Biddy had Ahni scoop a pot of snow from outside and set it over the fire to melt while they waited. When it was boiling hot, Biddy uncovered Jalmer's leg. Ahni took one look at the oozing pus and turned her back, gagging at the sight and the stench.

"Get over it," Biddy's voice was stern. "The drink makes him sleep, but he'll still feel a lot of pain when I begin to cut. I need you to straddle his chest. Face away from his legs so I don't have to put up with you fainting or something worse."

Then she set a cast iron skillet right over the fire. Ahni wondered why, but didn't have time to ask because Biddy said, "Ready? Up you go. Hold him steady no matter what. Pretend you're riding a horse when he bucks. And he will."

Ahni thought of running out the door and getting as far away as she could before darkness settled, but there was something about Old Biddy Bones. Deep in her own bones, Ahni knew that one did not disobey her.

CHAPTER 33

Ahni survived the cutting and sawing. She hoped Jalmer did, too. He had screamed, cried out, and tried to buck her off his chest. She had held his thrashing arms and tried to keep him as steady as she could. Once, she'd glanced back to see Old Biddy Bones with one foot on the floor and the other on the leg she was removing to keep it from kicking. The sound of the saw rasping its way through bone sent shudders up Ahni's spine! She fought hard to keep herself from retching.

Ahni almost did not survive what came next. Biddy took the iron skillet she'd heated on the fire and put it right on Jalmer's bleeding stump. Jalmer howled like a wolf caught in a trap, and Ahni fainted to the floor with a thud.

The stench of burned flesh still hung in the air when Biddy splashed a bucket of cold water on Ahni. "Up and at 'em. We have a patient to care for. No lying down on the job."

In her worst nightmares, Ahni had never so much as come close to anything like what had just happened.

"You must be tired. Guests sleep there." Old Biddy Bones pointed to a mossy corner. Ahni's feet were still sore, and she was troubled by what she'd just seen. She curled onto the moss and wrapped herself in the horse blanket and tried to muffle the sounds of Jalmer moaning. Throughout the night, Ahni woke often to see Biddy Bones plucking leaves and stems from the hanging bundles of plants. Then she forced spoonsful of herbal brew down Jalmer's throat. He moaned and struggled, but finally slept. It was then that Biddy herself climbed into the hammock. Ahni's tortured thoughts throughout the night fixated on getting away from this strange woman's hovel. She could follow the creek and hope it would lead her home. Home to Grammy.

The next morning, Biddy Bones pointed to Jalmer who squirmed on the table. "I still need your help today and maybe a few more days. You stay! You can start whittling him crutches. I'll feed him potions to ease his pain. If the infection has already spread beyond what we cut, then . . ." Old Biddy Bones did not finish the sentence.

Ahni felt a twinge of something. She didn't like the way Biddy looked at Jalmer. It reminded her of the man she'd seen in the tree watching the blanket toss when she'd first been at the logging camp. *Could it be?* Biddy had been surprised when Ahni called her a woman. She'd said she was sometimes a man, then changed the subject. Ahni inwardly shivered. Alfred had disappeared from the camp that same day, and some loggers blamed her for it. Ahni grew even more apprehensive, and her hands grew sweaty. *Why had Biddy said she'd been waiting for her?*

None of it made sense to Ahni, but she didn't have time for further thinking because Biddy handed her a basket made of twisted tamarack twigs. "Go collect buds from spruce trees and new sprays from the cedars. Also, be looking to see if any fiddle ferns are poking their heads up through the snow-covered duff yet. Look on hillsides where the sun shines."

Ahni didn't know what fiddle ferns were, but carefully scoured the soft ground where the snows had just melted. She found plenty of buds to pick from the trees and soon had a full basket. Fresh wolf and bear tracks ran down to the creek from the hill. Birds flitted from branches as Ahni felt the warm sun on her back. Shallow ponds formed in hollows where the snow was slowly melting. Crusty patches still stuck stubbornly in the shadows of trees. Ahni stretched in the sunlight and for a short while forgot about the sound of the saw scraping through bone.

Back in the rickety hut, Jalmer was worse. He thrashed! Yelled! Screamed! Cursed Old Biddy Bones for cutting off his leg! Biddy grabbed Ahni by the arm and told her to make sure Jalmer didn't pull the bloody rags off his stump while she concocted a stronger potion.

"Nothing works for him anymore. All I can do is brew the potion stronger and hope he settles down. If he doesn't . . ."

Ahni didn't like when Biddy didn't finish sentences. She could think of too many possible endings. Most of them not good! Images of an eclipse that hid the sun in the middle of the day, haunted her. *Was this all happening because she was born bad during an eclipse?* She didn't feel bad. She hadn't wanted the axe to chop into Jalmer's leg, or for Baby Moses to be born blue, or for the horses to drown, or anything else that had gone wrong at the logging camp. She vowed to herself to do what Mam had written for her. She would never, ever, again tell anyone about being born when the moon covered the sun.

Biddy handed Ahni a mash of roots and spruce tips along with a tin cup of steaming tea. "You must be hungry. Eat and drink now. Then rest!"

Ahni was hungry. She didn't know when she'd last eaten one of the wrinkled carrots or a chunk of bread. As she scooped mash into her mouth with her fingers, her hunger pains eased.

Old Biddy Bones ate, too, while she sat beside Ahni on the horse blanket and told her stories. Stories she said the wolves had told her.

"How do wolves tell stories?" Ahni asked.

"They tell them in wolf language. With lots of noises they make in their throats. Those sounds along with their tails, their ears, how they hold their heads, their paws, their whole posture, and even their eyes and tongues, are how they tell their stories. Sleep now and the wolves will tell you the story they told me."

Ahni wanted to ask more, but her eyelids were heavy—almost closing. She felt very weary.

"I wish you good dreams," Biddy said smiling.

Ahni fell fast into a sleep that was filled with a long wolf dream.

Long ago we wolves watched as a young she-person and he-person walked into our territory—the area we marked off with our piddle. No other wolf would dare cross our scent line, but two-legged humans know nothing of such things and would not respect them if they did know.

So, we watched to see what they would do. We hid in bushes. We hid behind trees. Two-leggeds do not know how to spot a wolf if the wolf does not want to be seen. The she-person rubbed her great belly and groaned. We wolves lifted our noses to scent her. It was not good. Everything told us that she was worried and in pain. She should have been lying on soft mosses and the he-person should have been waiting a short distance away ready to chase any dangers that threatened her.

Ahni stirred in her sleep. Old Biddy Bones spooned a potion into her mouth and wafted a smoking branch of herbs and roots under her nose, so she fell deeply asleep again to dream more of the story the wolves told.

Soon enough, the she-person lay gasping at the marshy edge of a great lake. The he-person looked on helplessly as she gave birth to a two-legged baby. He-person finally did something. He picked up the skinny, hairless, wailing newborn human. Instead of licking and cleaning the baby, he rubbed it with the hem of his shirt, then almost dropped the little one.

She-person scolded him for his carelessness, so he handed her the baby. She almost dropped it, too. Her only mouth-word was, "Noooooo!" His and her other language of sorrowful faces, droopy shoulders, and averted eyes told us wolves a deeply sad story as we watched.

Ahni wakened in the state where one is half-asleep and half-awake. She heard strange noises. Shuffling. Door opening. Old Biddy Bones spooned more warm liquid into Ahni's mouth and wafted the smoky branch for her to breathe again. Then Ahni heard nothing else as she fell into her wolf-story dream again.

He-person lifted she-person from the ground. Together they stood with their heads together as they looked at their baby lying in the reeds. They shook their heads, spoke no more in their mouth language, and pushed the baby closer to the murky waters of the marsh. Then they turned and quickly left our territory.

We wolves stayed hidden, waiting for the two-leggeds to return, to scoop up their baby, sniff it, cuddle it, and to take it with them. But that did not happen. We waited until we couldn't endure the crying and wailing a single moment longer. As the sun moved through the sky, two of our grandmother wolves gently nudged the baby from the muddy bank and onto soft mosses in the sunshine. Then the mother wolves gathered and let the baby suckle its fill. The little one made soft noises as its hunger faded.

Old Grey Wolf called a council. We gathered around and sniffed the scrawny, hairless, newborn. Then we studied it from head to toe. "Not he-person. Not she-person. No wolf had ever been born a not-he, not-she," said the oldest grandmother wolf. "Wonder if more two-leggeds are born that way." She gave the baby another sniff and walked away.

The wolves discussed what to do. "What every wolf has ever done and will forever do in the future," Old Grey said. "We do not let it die. We bring it into our pack." And so the wolves did. Soon the two-legged walked on hands and knees to become a four-legged, thinking it was a wolf itself. It learned the language of the pack and imitated their sounds, their sniffs, their postures to become one with them.

The dream ended. Ahni tried to fall back asleep. She wanted to know more about the person who had been raised by wolves. She clamped her eyes shut, but the dream did not return. She finally sat up and saw Old Biddy Bones scrubbing the table where Jalmer had lain. Bloody rags lay on the floor. Jalmer was nowhere to be seen.

"Where Jalmer go?" Ahni asked.

"Oh, you're awake. Too soon. Go back to sleep."

"Tried. Wanted more dream, but no more came. Where Jalmer?"

Biddy didn't answer, but stirred a huge kettle that hung over the fire. Ahni got up and stooped to go out the door to the crisscross logs that took the place of the slop pail she and Mam had used at the logging camp. "Don't go out yet. Have some tea. Relax and tell me your dream as we sip." She gave Ahni that unwavering stare that meant it was not the time to disobey.

The tea must have put Ahni back to sleep for a long time because when she awoke, there was no sign that Jalmer had ever lain on the table. The saw and bloody knives were clean and hanging from a branch. The blanket that had covered him was gone. His boot that he would have no more use for was no longer anywhere to be seen. The only things still there were Jalmer's coat and pants that hung in a corner and the crutch that Ahni had started to carve for him.

"Just let me put some of this root in the stew to thicken it. We'll have ourselves a delicious meal." Old Biddy Bones brushed a stray hair out of her eyes and smiled.

Ahni didn't like the smile. "Gotta go bad now." She rushed out to relieve herself before she soiled her clothes. Hunger clawed at her stomach. She planned to eat a big bowl of stew and then head for home. It didn't seem right that Jalmer had started for his home without his coat, pants, or even the half-made crutch to take the place of the leg that Biddy had sawed off. Ahni's empty stomach surged with sour bile just thinking about it.

CHAPTER 34

"Jalmer was feeling better. He wanted to go home. I gave him some roots to ease his pain before he hobbled off." Biddy explained when Ahni came back.

"Without jacket? No pants? Without crutch?" Ahni asked.

"He paid me for saving him by leaving his coat and pants. I found a nice straight branch he could use for a walking stick. He'll get along just fine. He's a strong man." Biddy threw the half-made crutch into her fire before filling two bowls with stew.

Ahni didn't like the explanation. It didn't seem right, but she was hungry so she stirred the broth. Big chunks of meat, leaves, and root floated around. The stew in her bowl was different than anything she'd ever had. No potatoes, carrots, or rutabaga. Just meat, leaves, and root. Next time, she'd give Biddy one of the carrots Matti and Kalle had brought her, but there would be no next time. After she ate, she was definitely heading home to Grammy.

"This deer meat?" she asked picking a piece up with her fingers.

Old Biddy Bones looked startled. "Of course!" Then she bent her head to scoop some stew into her own mouth.

"How you get deer meat for stew?" Ahni asked dropping the piece back into her bowl.

"Plenty easy if you know how."

"You have gun?"

"No need if you know how."

"Tell me."

"First, tell me about your dream." Old Biddy Bones wiped her mouth on her sleeve.

"It was wolf dream. Like wolves tellin' me story."

"Tell me what they told you, and I'll tell you more."

"What more there be to tell?"

Old Biddy Bones' voice sounded edgy and annoyed when she said, "Get on with your dream."

Ahni felt Biddy's irritation, so she told about the baby abandoned by its parents and how a pack of wolves took care of the two-legged child. When she finished, she chewed on the last bit of tough meat, sipped the last mouthful of broth in her bowl, and said, "Wanted more sleep. More dream. Find out what happen to baby."

Biddy's face softened as she said, "I can tell you what happened. I was that baby—unwanted because I was different. Raised by wolves. And now I live here. Alone, except when someone needs healing, or is lost."

Raised by wolves? After Big Thunder died, Pap had said he should have brought Ahni to the forest for the wolves to do what they would with her as soon as she was born. She'd always thought the wolves would have eaten her, but maybe they would have cared for her as they had for Old Biddy Bones.

Thoughts tumbled through Ahni's mind. Biddy had been unwanted and abandoned. The same as herself. Different because she was born during an eclipse. Born bad and abandoned to a logging camp by Pap. Abandoned by Mam who wanted to go down the river on a wanigan with Harry. At least she had Grammy, or hoped that Grammy still wanted her. If not, she would go into the forest and live with wolves.

"How you learn healing?" Ahni asked. "Everyone say you good healer."

"Ah, that. The knowing came to me long ago when I had just begun my full moon blood flows."

"How that be?" Ahni had no idea what the full moon blood flows were. They sounded awful to her, but she wanted to know about the healing.

"One day, I heard a sorrowful yipping so followed the sound into the dense forest. I found a soft-eyed wolf pup at the edge of a boggy lake. The whole family pack surrounded the wounded one. Bloody fur marked a hole in the wolf's shoulder. *Hunter!* The mother wolf licked the open wound and looked at me as if to say, *See how cruel the hunters are who bring fire sticks into our woods?*

"The sun pierced the thickness of the forest and shone on the young wolf. The pup moaned and closed its eyes. The mother wolf licked harder and looked at me for help. I sat myself next to the pup feeling helpless. *What could I do?* My skin tingled from head to toe. I thought it was fear because I didn't know how to help. The wolves had raised me. Been kind to me."

Old Biddy Bones wiped her eyes on her sleeve and was quiet for a long time. Finally, she started telling her story again. "In my distress, I pulled at a clump of moss that surrounded me. My hands tingled. It seemed a natural thing to do so I pressed the clump of moss to the pup's shoulder. Mother wolf sniffed it. Looked at the me. Sniffed again, and then licked the bloody spot on the other side of the pup's shoulder where the bullet had left his body. I tugged at another handful of moss and pressed that to the other gaping hole. Mother wolf sniffed again. She, with her paw, and I, with my hand, pressed the wads of moss tightly covering the two wounds on the pup's shoulder."

Old Biddy Bones paused again. A faraway look clouded her eyes. "It was so long ago," she began again. "We—the wolf pack and I sat together as the sun coursed the sky and night fell. Every once in a while, I pulled fresh clumps of moss to press against the gaping wounds. Mother wolf and I held them in place. Other wolves from the pack circled and watched. A day later, or maybe it was two or three, the young wolf whimpered, then shakily stood. The moss dropped to the ground. He waded into the shallows of the lake to drink. Mother wolf nudged me with her nose so I crawled through the moss to the water's edge to drink, too. Mother wolf followed. Her pup was whole again. He would not die.

"From that day on, I watched what the animals of the woods ate, what they would not eat, what bark and roots they chewed when giving birth. What berries and leaves they ate when they walked with a limp. I watched, learned, and made harmless potions and thick poultices. As the years passed, I came to know that the tingling in my hands meant a mixture was good. I also learned that sharp pricks meant a plant could be deadly if used the wrong way. I tried my potions on the hunters I captured. That way, I learned about mixtures that were good, and mixtures that were not."

Ahni and Old Biddy Bones sat quietly for a long time. Ahni studied the many bunches of roots, leaves, flowers, and berries that hung from the hut's ceiling. She wondered if her own hands would tingle or would they prick when she reached to pluck leaves for a brew.

Still having so many questions to ask, Ahni finally broke the silence. "You learn lots from the wolves. How you learn human talk?" she asked.

"First, I'll tell you other things I learned from the wolves. One of the best things I learned was to sniff. You can learn a lot by sniffing. You can smell fear, anger, sickness, and so many other things. When I was very young, but too old to suckle, I watched a young pup nuzzled the mouth of a wolf that'd been out hunting. When the wolf burped up meat into the pup's mouth, I learned to do the same. Later on, I learned how to hunt small animals along with the wolves so I didn't have to depend on what they brought me. I learned to bite through the fur of the rabbits, voles, and squirrels so I could eat the guts and flesh. I don't have sharp fangs like wolves, so it was much harder for me."

Ahni was fascinated, but revolted to think of eating food out of a wolf's mouth and eating everything raw. "But how you learn people talk?"

"Be patient. I'll get there. As I grew, the wolves pulled things off clothes lines from farm houses so I had something to wear other than the furs of animals they caught. When I was no longer small enough to crawl into their dens in hollow trees or dug under thickets, they brought me to this high hill where I'd be close to the creek. They watched me build this hut from branches and downed trees. They even carried branches in their mouths to help me. Some of the young wolves dug moss for that corner you sleep in. They told me in their wolf language that I would have everything I needed on this high hill."

"But how you learn human talk?"

Biddy scowled at Ahni, so she stroked her pouch and waited patiently for the rest of Biddy's story. "At first, the wolves brought me to small farms carved out in the woods. They hid me among bushes so I could watch the two-leggeds and listen to them talk. I didn't learn much that way, but I at least tried to imitate their sounds. Later on, when I already lived here, I started capturing lost hunt-ers—men with rifles on their shoulders, looking to shoot a deer or maybe even a wolf. I offered them food and a place to rest. I gave them tea made of the sleep-ing root. Then I kept them tied up real good. Little by little I learned their words and language. At first it was just things like 'Let me go, you wretched witch' or something else not so nice."

"When did you let lost hunters go?"

"Who said I let them go? I needed food. They kept me well-fed."

"They hunted an' brought you deer or rabbit?"

"As you say. As you say." Old Biddy Bones laughed and got that look in her eye I remembered seeing when I saw the man in the trees while bouncing high dur-ing the blanket toss.

"You spied on people to learn. You ever in tall tree watchin' at loggin' camp?"

"More than once, and I saw you flying in the air. I thought I'd like to know a reaI human girl who laughed as she was tossed so high."

"That same day, Alfred went missin'. I got blamed cuz I told I saw strange man in tree. Some loggers ask over an' over what I did to him. You take Alfred?"

"Alfred? I never ask names, but I remember him. He smelled of wood smoke and pine. His behind smelled of beans and venison. He was like all the others—didn't like when I sniffed his butt. I have to remember that's a wolf thing. Humans don't like it. They don't even like being sniffed anywhere. If they only knew what's learned from a good sniffing, they'd do it, too."

"What happen Alfred? He never came back to camp. He stay here and feed you, too?"

"You might say so. Better yet, I got—or I should say—he had a saw with him that was useful for taking off Jalmer's leg."

"So, you were man I saw in tree."

"I spied on the camp many more times, but you didn't see me. I was careful."

"You *Wiindigoo*? Take children? Eat them?"

Old Biddy Bones laughed. "I'm not *Wiindigoo*, or any other creature people make up."

Ahni settled onto her horse blanket. Old Biddy Bones had answered so many of her questions, even what had happened to Alfred. She tried to imagine being raised by wolves. Learning their language. Learning human language. She smiled to think of people sniffing other people like dogs and cats and wolves do to each other. She had one more question.

"You give leafy packet to man who bring Jalmer here? What in packet?"

"Oh, that." Old Biddy Bones scratched her underarms, then her scalp. "I warned that man. Just a pinch. A tiny pinch is all he'd need. He wanted more than a pinch. Said he might need more. So, I ground enough of the root, then added berries to ease pain. It was enough for several pinches."

"What he say it for?"

"For a woman who needed to give birth right away—before the snow melted. I warned him that a little was better than more. Early births aren't good, and too much could be dangerous."

"Harry gave all pinches to Mam. Baby born blue an' die." Ahni felt a hitch in her voice. It still saddened her to think of the little boy who should have been her Baby Brother Moses who'd grow and run and play and laugh with her.

Old Biddy Bones didn't say anything for a while. "Wolves are never born blue. I've never heard of it. So strange. Some births are strange. Like mine. Like yours when the sky turned dark in the middle of the day."

Ahni perked up. "How you know I 'clipse born?"

"Overheard loggers talking another day when I spied on the logging camp, looking for food and maybe an axe. And that man you call Jalmer told me about you, too. They blamed you for all the bad things that happened. I wanted to know the girl who was born peculiar like I was. But you're not that way at all. I'd never seen a human girl up close and was curious. The first time you slept here, I sniffed you good and looked you all over."

Biddy Bones paused. Her voice turned wistful. "You're different than I am. And I'm different than Alfred and Jalmer. I'm different than everyone. My wolves accepted me as I was. My parents didn't. Unfortunately, those old wolves who cared for me and taught me all died long ago. The new ones don't care about me."

What Biddy said made Ahni think of Pap, Harry, and all the others who didn't want her. She understood why Biddy lived by herself deep into the forest. She patted the pouch White Wolf had given her. *Stone. I be strong. Pine cone. I protect what good inside me. Manoomen. I grow food. Never be hungry.*

"The weather is warming." Old Biddy Bones said, "When summer days are longest, and the moon is its fullest, the wolves all around here will join with other packs. They will lift their heads to the moon and howl the night through. The old wolves used to call to me in the moonlight, inviting me to join them. The younger ones dance in the shadows, but never call to me. I follow their pack and watch them from behind trees anyway. I am no longer allowed to sing to the moon with them. I am no longer part of a pack or part of the wolf family because I am two-legged." Biddy's voice grew sadder and almost so soft that Ahni couldn't hear her.

The two sat together thinking of how they didn't belong. Finally, Old Biddy Bones rose and without a word, made some tea for Ahni.

CHAPTER 35

While watching the girl sleep, Old Biddy Bones' eyes rested on the pouch the girl fondled so often. Wondering what was so treasured, Biddy Bones carefully untied it from around the girl's neck and shook everything out. A stone. A pine cone. A scrap of singed cloth. And some seeds.

Old Biddy Bones scratched her head. Picking up each of the items in turn, she wondered why the girl cherished those plain old things—things that should have just been left on the forest floor or thrown into a stream. She put everything back. Stroking it as the girl had, she liked the soft smooth feel so she tied the pouch around her own neck and hid it under her shirt.

As the girl continued sleeping, Old Biddy Bones picked leaves, berries, and roots. Her hand was steady, and her fingers tingled slightly telling her that each one she chose was the right one. As she ground everything into a mash, she thought of one lost hunter who had pleaded with her when he realized that she didn't plan to let him go. "My wife and children need me. Love me. I need to go home to them. To care for them. I love them."

That hunter's eyes had become soft and teary. He was the only hunter she'd ever let go.

It had also been the first time Old Biddy Bones had heard the word *love*. She was sure she knew what it meant. She had loved the old wolves and missed them every day. When Ahni told her about Grammy, her eyes softened and her voice became gentle. Ahni loved her Grammy.

Biddy had always let the sick and wounded go after she'd healed them. They'd been different from the hunters. They were more like the wolf pup she'd first healed long ago. The sick and wounded thanked her for her care. They'd asked if they could help her in some way when they were better. Their eyes and voices had been warm when they spoke to her.

Lost hunters who stumbled upon her hut were brash and demanding. They expected her to feed them and let them warm by her fire. She'd drugged them. Tied them up. Kept them captive while she learned what she needed from them. They hated her, feared her, and couldn't wait to be away from her. Their eyes and voices had never been soft.

Old Biddy Bones had already kept the girl under the spell of potions for two full moons. Another moon was growing in the night sky. She liked Ahni's company. Whenever the girl had talked about leaving, Old Biddy Bones had made a potion— a special potion that tingled her fingers and took away the girl's desire to leave. Then, sitting in the light of the moon each night, the two of them had told each other stories. She told wolf stories. Ahni told of the flying horse Pegagus, and of a boy named David and the giant Goliath. Biddy liked hearing the story about the crow that taught people about the life-giving sap of the maple tree. More than once, the girl recounted a story about the chipmunk that made the sun rise and shine. When Ahni told of the men who treated her poorly and sent her away from the logging camp, Old Biddy Bones shuddered. The stories she'd told about Pap and Mam abandoning her made Old Biddy Bones' tears fall. She herself had been abandoned by her mother and father, too. The longer the girl stayed, the fonder Biddy became of her and wanted her company.

Biddy's heart ached when she told stories of how the old wolves had cleaned her the same way they cleaned their pups. She still missed their soft licks on her cheeks, her forehead, behind her ears. She missed how they sat with her, lay by her, and played chasing games with her and the pups. She missed the softness in their eyes when they looked at her. It was the same softness they used with their own. But those wolves were all gone now.

Old Biddy Bones thought back to all the days and nights she'd given the girl potions that would keep her ensnared and unable to leave. She dreamed of Ahni staying with her forever. She imagined the walks they'd take through the woods. Of the berries they'd pick. Of the bird songs they'd listen to. Of the fresh mushrooms they'd pick after a rain. With a pang in her heart, Old Biddy Bones realized that could never be. She wanted the girl's company, but she was like the old wolves—her days on the hill would soon be over. She needed to let the girl go. The girl loved Grammy. Grammy loved and called the girl *Dear, Sweet Lamb-i-kins* in return.

Biddy wondered what her human name would have been if her own parents hadn't abandoned her. The girl had called her Old Biddy Bones. That name was as good as any. Her wolf family had named her *Two legs-slow runner.* They said it with their ears forward and a slow swish of their tails. The young wolves just laid their ears back and lifted a lip when they saw her. She understood that to mean *Not wolf. Keep away.*

Carefully, Biddy stirred the mash into hot water for a forgetting potion—one she'd accidentally discovered when trying to concoct a mixture that would endear herself to one of her captives.

She sang as she mixed. Her voice rasped as tears slid down her cheeks.
Child Born of an Eclipse,
Remember not
Old Biddy Bones and the taking of Jalmer's leg.
Remember not
Stories the wolves told.
Remember not
The haunts of Old Biddy Bones.
As you wend your way home, listen for the tune you know so well.
But, remember not
Your days and nights with Old Biddy Bones.

Ahni turned in her sleep. Old Biddy Bones put a hand to her shoulder and gently calmed her. The pouch lay cold and prickly against her own chest. As she patted the girl's shoulder, she decided to give the pouch back. Biddy stroked it, untied it, then curled it around the girl's neck. Feeling the pouch warm and tingle softly on the girl, she knew she'd done the right thing. Her voice broke as she murmured, "Rest now. Your journey is ahead. Mine is almost over. Remember not Old Biddy Bones."

CHAPTER 36

After feeding the potion to Ahni, Old Biddy Bones led the drowsy girl to the creek at the bottom of the hill. She lay her on soft mosses and covered her with the horse blanket. Tears streamed down her cheeks as she whispered into the girl's ear, "Remember not."

Then she struggled her way back up the hill and followed a crooked path into the woods. At the top, she paused to catch her breath. Finally, she lifted her chin and howled. A long, low howl. A howl to call wolves to her. Leaning against a gnarled tree, she waited. A long time passed. She howled again. After another long wait, she heard the soft padding of feet. A branch snapped. Then she saw a shadow slide behind a tree. Then another. She waited without saying a word. When she heard a soft snuffling, she stepped out of the shadows and lowered herself on knees and elbows. She lowered her head almost to the ground showing she was weak, submissive, and asking for help. Two wolves stepped closer. Ruffs raised. Watchful.

In a soft whisper and in the language of wolves, Biddy told of the young girl asleep by the creek. Of how she needed protection and care so she could find her Grammy and home. She ended by telling the wolves, "I am old. My days in these woods are short. I ask this, not for myself, but for the girl."

The wolves lowered their ruffs, sniffed the prone woman, then turned to find the girl.

As Ahni slept, water rippled over the stones of the small creek. A bird fluttered overhead bringing a bug to hatchlings in its nest. Ahni didn't hear or see any of those things. She didn't feel a wolf curl close to her back or feel the one curved at her stomach. She dreamed of breathing tangy aromas. She dreamed of sun rises and sun sets. She heard words breathed into her ear. *Forget all that happened high on the hill. Follow the creek to your people.*

Ahni dreamed that a pack of wolves called to her. Their howls echoed in the night. Eerie and beautiful. She wanted to answer their call. She wanted to dance among the shadowy trees with wolves. She wanted to follow their tracks, but a breath in her ear said, "*Go now. To Grammy.*"

Ahni finally awoke to the sounds of the stream trickling over rocks and squirrels chattering in the trees. She stretched and looked around. A fine mist hung in the air. She shook her head trying to clear her vision.

Where was she? The last thing she remembered was trudging along river banks and winding her way around trees in the forest. Her feet were sore and her stomach growled for another chunk of bread or bite of apple. The sun was low. Lost, she needed to find a place to spend the night. A high hill had loomed in front of her beckoning to her. As she looked up at the hill, she no longer felt the urge to climb it. She remembered being tired and foot-sore, but she didn't remember settling to spend the night by the narrow creek.

She stood to get her bearings. She shook her head again. Yesterday, when she'd stood at the base of the hill, snow still crusted most of the ground in an early thaw. Spring was just beginning. Now, everything around her was in full bloom. Little violets and other flowers blossomed in abundance. Leaves quaked in the soft breeze. Everything was the fresh green of full summer. The sun had strength. She bent to the creek to scoop water into her mouth. Tiny frogs hopped along the bank. How had that happened as she slept? It took a long time in the spring for tadpoles to become frogs.

Only been one night! I so tired I slept two? Even one or two nights weren't enough for tadpoles to change. Trees didn't leaf out that fast. The sun couldn't have moved higher into the sky that fast either. Try as she could, Ahni could not figure out where so many days had gone. Was she still dreaming? She held her hands to her head and tried to remember.

Not only did the whole woods around her seem wrong, but Ahni felt as though there was a hole in her memory. She was forgetting something that had been real. She looked up the steep hill. She didn't feel a tug to climb it now.

She muttered to herself, "It time. I follow creek an' hope it leads to Grammy. First, I eat."

She reached for the bundle where she'd wrapped the loaf of bread Mam had given her and the carrots and apples some of the loggers had secretly brought her. A little mouse scampered out of the bundle. The loaf of bread had gone moldy and was chewed on by the mouse. Maybe many mice. It was only one long day and two nights since the bread had been pulled out of the great oven in the cook shack. *How had it gotten so moldy?*

Ahni tossed the loaf into the trees and shook the bundle. No carrots or apples fell out. She knew she hadn't eaten all of them the day she'd walked until her feet hurt. Again, she shook her head to clear her thinking, but no amount of shaking could help her make any sense of what had happened to her.

Puzzled, Ahni took one last look up the steep hill, wondering what was hiding in the wavering shadows. She put her hand to feel for the pouch Big John, White Wolf, and Cloudy had given her. The stone warmed under her hand. It gave her strength, but feelings of strangeness were still there.

Still bewildered, she tried to think only of going home to Grammy. Shouldering the horse blanket, she set off following the creek. Every once in a while, a flash of a broken image flickered somewhere in her head. A shimmer of a face, a glint of a hammock, a misty trace of a bowl of stew, an empty boot. Nothing made sense. Then, in an instant, the image would be gone and forgotten.

If Ahni had not been a two-legged human, she would have known to look behind herself as she walked the rocky shore of the creek. Gliding silently from tree to tree were two wolves watching her every step, padding softly behind her. They stopped when she stopped. They lapped clear waters after she'd had her fill. They sniffed her tracks. They even sniffed the wet spot where she squatted behind a tree.

Along the way, Ahni picked ripe strawberries and plucked spruce tips to eat. She remembered to give thanks to the Great Creator like Big John had told her. When, at last, the sky darkened after a long day, Ahni found a hollow under a huge pine tree. There she spread her blanket and settled for the night. Before falling asleep, she looked to the skies. She wished to find Pegasus flying above her in the stars, but Grammy had told her that Pegasus was only visible in the autumn skies. She held her pouch for comfort.

A low howling followed by joyful yips woke her from the depths of her slumber. A full moon shone in the black star-speckled sky above her. Soon the air was filled with the distant songs of many packs of wolves celebrating the fullness of summer—a chorus of wolves. Ahni imagined them yipping and howling as they leapt, played and nipped each other's ears. She wondered what it would be like to be there with them, playing and rolling in the summer grass. The howling of the wolves brought a flashing image to her. *What was it about wolves she should know?* A thought fluttered like a moth, but escaped from her memory each time she tried to capture it. That night she dreamed two wolves lay beside her.

Rested and happy that she'd had such a wonderful wolf dream during the night, Ahni set out at a fast pace. Her dreams of happy wolf families made her lonesome for Grammy.

That morning, the sun shone brightly, and birds sang as they fluttered from tree to tree. By mid-afternoon when the sun was high in the sky, Ahni heard a melody she remembered from a long time ago. *Pium paum. The cradle rocks for the innocent child . . .* She began to hum along. Then she saw a ragged woman, bent and walking with a stick. She carried a bundle on her back and stumbled on the bumpy path. Ahni hurried toward her, thinking to help carry the bundle and to ask for directions. As she got closer, she heard the woman singing again. Ahni quickened her steps remembering that Grammy had sung *Pium paum* to her.

"Grammy." She hesitated, fearful the woman would be someone she didn't know.

The woman stopped and dropped her bundle.

"Grammy?" Ahni's voice was a ragged whisper. The woman looked so much older and fragile than she remembered Grammy.

The woman held her arms wide and gasped. "My Dear, Sweet Lamb-i-kins! You've come back to me!"

Ahni ran into the welcoming arms. "Grammy." She sobbed over and over again. Ahni felt Grammy's heart beat against her own chest. She felt Grammy's tears join with her own tears. Grammy's arms held her tightly, and she held onto Grammy, never wanting to let her go.

Two wolves watched. They sniffed the air and then slowly disappeared into the woods.

ACKNOWLEDGEMENTS

I owe a big thank you to the Carlton County Historical Society, especially to Anja Bottila and Carol Klitzke who led me to articles and photographs of the early logging days and camps.

A special thanks goes to Michelle Goose and Stephanie DeFoe Hammit (Late President of the Fond du Lac Tribal and Community College), who helped with Ojibwe words and names. All errors of usage are my own.

I am also thankful for my writing group for their help and encouragement throughout the years.

Without the support and "push" from my husband Dale, this and my other books would still be collecting dust deep in my computer files. He truly is Mighty Mouse because he often does "Come to save the day!" Thank you!

OJIBWE GLOSSARY

AANAKWAD a cloud

WAABISHK-AANAKWAD White Cloud

WAABISHKI-MA'IINGAN White Wolf

GIIWEDIN-ANANG Northstar

NIMAAMAA my mother (what most people use nowadays)

NOOS my father (older terms for father)

NIBAABAA my father (modern version)

OOSAN his/her father

WIINDIGOO cannibal monster. Wiindigoo is considered very scary and people usually avoid saying (or even writing) the name

Reference: Ojibwe People's dictionary, https://ojibwe.lib.umn.edu

I've always been fascinated by myths, legends, and fiction that depict feral children, especially those reared by wild animals such as wolves, apes, monkeys, and bears. Famous examples include *Romulus and Remus*, Rudyard Kipling's *Mowgli*, and Edgar Rice Burroughs's *Tarzan*.

In my research I found an intriguing story about Amala and Kamala who were allegedly feral girls of Bengal, India, raised by a wolf family.

Superstitions are a way humans try to explain the inexplicable. They play an important role in *Born of an Eclipse*. It is easy to scoff at such beliefs, but how many hotels do not have a 13th floor? Or have you ever said something like *Knock on wood*?

1. Discuss the possible origins of stories about feral children who are raised by animals.

2. What are the roles of superstitions and omens in our lives.

3. Folktales and *Bible* stories are told throughout the book. What is their significance, especially to Ahni?

4. What is the importance of Mam and Ahni playing "Cat's Cradle" and the following lines from Chapter 21? *Ahni looked at Mam who twisted her fingers together and shook her head. Ahni tried to pull the right strings to make the Witch's Broom, but Mam dropped all the strings. Ahni picked them up. Everything was knotted. She tried to straighten the string, but the knots were too tight. She'd never get them right again. Maybe nothing would be right again.*

5. What is the significance, if any, of the cradle song that Grammy sings, *Pium Paum. The cradle rocks for the innocent child. . . .*

6. What is the role of Old Biddy Bones?

7. Was Ahni *born bad*? What evidence is there that she was or wasn't?

FURTHER READING

1. Internet searches using key words: Feral child(ren), Raised by wolves, Omens, Superstitions.

2. Internet searches for photos of logging camps, wanigans, cook shacks, etc.

3. *Pium paum.* Finnish Children's song. (May be heard on-line.)

4. *Julie of the Wolves.* Jean Craighead George. Harper Collins. 1972.

5. *The Little People and the Water of Life.* Ronda J. Snow. Black Bears & Blueberries Publishing. 2021.

6. *The Spirit of the North Wind.* Anthony Anselmo. Black Bears & Blueberries Publishing. 2023.

Katharine Johnson lives in Northern Minnesota with her husband and a flock of wild turkeys. The woodlands with all the critters that come to their yard provide inspiration and setting for most of her stories.

Her four published books have brought her on journeys of self-discovery. *The Mukluk Ball* is a fun picture book. *The Wind and the Drum*, a historical fiction novel, was selected as the 2018 One Book Northland. *Born in a Red Canoe* was a finalist for the 2023 Minnesota Book Award. *Sylvie's Silence* has been accepted as a nominee for the 2023 Northeast Minnesota Book Award.

She has also published several short stories, biographies, and poetry in anthologies. One children's story "Company's Here" was published in the *Ladybug* children's magazine. Her short story "Ada" won the Jonis Agee Fiction Award.

She is a member of SCBWI, Lake Superior Writers, and a local writers' group.

Much of her "shelter in place" time was spent reading scads of MG and YA books to deeply explore those exciting fields of literature.